Herbert Ward

Five Years with the Congo Cannibals

Third Edition

Herbert Ward

Five Years with the Congo Cannibals
Third Edition

ISBN/EAN: 9783337237691

Printed in Europe, USA, Canada, Australia, Japan

Cover: Foto ©Andreas Hilbeck / pixelio.de

More available books at **www.hansebooks.com**

Sincerely Yours
Herbert Ward

FIVE YEARS

WITH THE

CONGO CANNIBALS

BY

HERBERT WARD

ILLUSTRATED BY THE AUTHOR, BY VICTOR PERARD, & W. B. DAVIS

THIRD EDITION

London
CHATTO & WINDUS, PICCADILLY
1891

PRINTED BY
SPOTTISWOODE AND CO., NEW-STREET SQUARE
LONDON

I AM MY MOTHER'S FIRST-BORN.

MY TWELVE YEARS' ADVENTURES IN UNCIVILIZED LANDS
HAVE CAUSED HER MUCH ANXIETY.

TO HER

I DEDICATE THIS BOOK.

H. W.

CONTENTS.

PART I.
LOWER CONGO.

CHAPTER V.

CHAPTER VI.

CHAPTER VII.

CHAPTER VIII.

CHAPTER IX.

CHAPTER X.

PART II.

UPPER CONGO.

CHAPTER VI.

CHAPTER VII.

CHAPTER VIII.

CHAPTER IX.

CHAPTER X.

CHAPTER XI.

CHAPTER XII.

PART III.

CANOE JOURNEYS.

CHAPTER VI.

CHAPTER VII.

LIST OF ILLUSTRATIONS.

PREFACE

a

PREFACE.

WITH pen and pencil I collected, from 1884 until 1889, a few details and phases of everyday life among the uncivilised races of Congo-land.

Having familiarised myself with the three most popular languages of a portion of that country—the Kikongo, spoken by the Lower Congo tribes; the Kibangi, of the Upper Congo; and Kiswahili, the language of Tippo Tib's Arab followers at Stanley Falls—I was in a position to obtain information direct from the people.

During those years I was the recipient of much generous hospitality from many Europeans, particularly the Baptist missionaries, Mr. and Mrs. Ingham, Mr. and Mrs. Clarke, Mr. Grenfell, and Mr. Bentley.

The recollection of my many friends and companions on the Congo will ever afford the brightest landmark of my life in Africa. But, alas! many of those friends have been stricken down with fever and now lie buried there, others are still toiling there, and the remainder are scattered about the world.

In the spring of 1887, while still in Africa, I became a member of Mr. Henry M. Stanley's Emin Pacha Relief Expedition, and was subsequently one of the five officers in Yambuya Camp on the Aruimi River.

As the subject-matter of this volume is confined to matters illustrative of native life in Congo-land, a brief outline of my connection with some of the tragic events which befell this portion of Mr. Stanley's expedition, known as the Rear Guard, may not be considered out of place.

In May 1887 the Emin Pacha Relief Expedition embarked on the Upper Congo, the overland march through the cataract region of the Lower Congo being completed. By the deficiency of accommodation on board the three river steamers in which the expedition embarked, a large proportion of the loads of ammunition, merchandise, &c., was left at Stanley Pool, in charge of Mr. J. Rose Troup, and a temporary camp containing 125 men " weakest in body " was formed at Bolobo, about 150 miles further up the Congo, and left in command of myself and Mr. William Bonny until the river steamer of the Congo State, *Le Stanley,* returned for us. On August 14 we three, with our men and loads, landed in Yambuya Camp on the Aruimi River, about 1,500 miles from the Atlantic coast. This camp of the Rear Guard was in command of Major E. M. Barttelot and Mr. J. S. Jameson, with a residue of 127 Zanzibaris and Soudanese, after the 383 men had been selected for the Advanced Guard under Mr. Stanley, who had started on the march to Emin Pacha June 28, six weeks previous to our arrival, and since that date no further news from Mr. Stanley ever reached Yambuya Camp.

Immediately upon our arrival, after handing over our men and stores to Major Barttelot, we read the following letter of instructions written by Mr. Stanley before his departure :—

To Major Barttelot, &c.

June 21, 1887

Sir,—As the senior of those officers accompanying me on the Emin Pacha Relief Expedition, the command of this important post naturally devolves on you. It is also for the interest of the expedition that you accept this command, from the fact that your Soudanese company, being soldiers, and more capable of garrison duty than the Zanzibaris, will be better utilised than on the road.

The steamer *Stanley* left Yambuya on the 22nd of this month for Stanley Pool. If she meets with no mischance she ought to be at Leopoldville on July 2. In two days more she will be loaded with about 500 loads of our goods, which were left in charge of Mr. J. R. Troup. This gentleman will embark, and on July 4 I assume that the *Stanley* will commence her ascent of the river, and arrive at Bolobo on the 9th. Fuel being ready, the 125 men in charge of Messrs. Ward and Bonny, now at Bolobo, will embark, and the steamer will continue her journey. She will be at Bangala on July 19, and arrive here on July 31. Of course, the lowness of the river in that month may delay her a few days, but having great confidence in her captain, you may certainly expect her before August 10.[1]

It is the non-arrival of these goods and men which compels me to appoint you as commander of this post. But as I shall shortly expect the arrival of a strong reinforcement of men,[2] greatly exceeding the Advance Force, which must, at all hazards, push on to the rescue of Emin Pacha, I hope you will not be detained longer than a few days after the departure of the *Stanley* on her final return to Stanley Pool in August.

Meantime, pending the arrival of our men and goods, it behoves you to be very alert and wary in the command of this stockaded camp. Though the camp is favourably situated and naturally strong, a brave enemy would find it no difficult task to capture if the commander is lax in discipline, vigour, and energy. Therefore I feel sure that I have made a wise choice in selecting you to guard our interests here during our absence.

The interests now entrusted to you are of vital importance to this expedition. The men you will eventually have under you consist of more than an entire third of the expedition. The goods that will be brought up are the currency needed for transit through the regions beyond the lakes; there will be a vast store of ammunition and provisions, which are of equal

---

[1] She arrived on August 14. Had been detained a few days by running on a snag.

[2] Tippo Tib's 600 carriers.

importance to us. The loss of these men and goods would be
certain ruin to us, and the Advance Force itself would need to
solicit relief in its turn. Therefore, weighing this matter well,
I hope you will spare no pains to maintain order and discipline in your camp, and make your defences complete, and
keep them in such a condition that however brave an enemy
may be he can make no impression on them. For this latter
purpose I would recommend you to make an artificial ditch six
feet wide, three feet deep, leading from the natural ditch,
where the spring is round the stockade. A platform like that
on the southern side of the camp, constructed near the eastern
as well as at the western gate, would be of advantage to the
strength of the camp. For remember, it is not the natives
alone who may wish to assail you, but the Arabs and their
followers may, through some cause or other, quarrel with you
and assail your camp.

Our course from here will be due east, or by magnetic
compass east by south as near as possible. Certain marches
that we may make may not exactly lead in the direction aimed
at. Nevertheless, it is the south-west corner of Lake Albert,
near or at Kavalli, that is our destination. When we arrive
there we shall form a strong camp in the neighbourhood,
launch our boat, and steer for Kibero, in Unyoro, to hear from
Signor Casati, if he is there, of the condition of Emin Pacha. If
the latter is alive and in the neighbourhood of the lake we shall
communicate with him, and our after conduct must be guided by
what we shall learn of the intentions of Emin Pacha. We may

assume that we shall not be longer than a fortnight with him before deciding on our return toward the camp along the same road traversed by us.

We will endeavour, by blazing trees and cutting saplings along our road, to leave sufficient traces of the route taken by us. We shall always take, by preference, tracks leading eastward. At all crossings where paths intersect we shall hoe up and make a hole a few inches deep across all paths not used by us, besides blazing trees when possible.

It may happen, should Tippo Tib have sent the full number of adults promised by him to me, viz. 600 men (able to carry loads), and the *Stanley* has arrived safely with the 125 men left by me at Bolobo, that you will feel yourself sufficiently competent to march the column, with all the goods brought by the *Stanley*, and those left by me at Yambuya, along the road pursued by me. In that event, which would be very desirable, you will follow closely our route, and before many days we should most assuredly meet. No doubt you will find our bomas intact and standing, and you should endeavour to make your marches so that you could utilise these as you marched. Better guides than those bomas of our route could not be made. If you do not meet them in the course of two days' march, you may rest assured that you are not on our route.

It may happen also that though Tippo Tib has sent some men, he has not sent enough to carry the goods with your own force. In that case you will, of course, use your discretion as

to what goods you can dispense with to enable you to march.
For this purpose you should study your list attentively.

1st. Ammunition, especially fixed, is most important.

2nd. Beads, brass wire, cowries and cloth rank next.

3rd. Private luggage.

4th. Powder and caps.

5th. European provisions.

6th. Brass rods as used on the Congo.

7th. Provisions (rice, beans, peas, millet, biscuits).

Therefore you must consider, after rope, sacking, tools, such
as shovels (never discard an axe or bill-hook), how many sacks
of provisions you can distribute among your men to enable
you to march, whether half the brass rods in the boxes could
not go also, and there stop. If you still cannot march, then it
would be better to make two marches of six miles twice over,
if you prefer marching to staying for our arrival, than throw
too many things away.

With the *Stanley's* final departure from Yambuya, you
should not fail to send a report to Mr. William Mackinnon,
care of Gray, Dawes, & Co., 13 Austin Friars, London, of what
has happened at your camp in my absence, or when I started
away eastward; whether you have heard of or from me at all,
when you do expect to hear, and what you purpose doing.
You should also send a true copy of this order, that the Relief
Committee may judge for themselves whether you have acted,
or propose to act, judiciously.

Your present garrison shall consist of eighty rifles, and

from forty to fifty supernumeraries. The *Stanley* is to bring
you within a few weeks fifty more rifles and seventy-five
supernumeraries, under Messrs. Troup, Ward, and Bonny.

I associate Mr. J. S. Jameson with you at present. Messrs.
Troup, Ward, and Bonny will submit to your authority. In
the ordinary duties of the defence, and the conduct of the camp
or of the march, there is only one chief, which is yourself; but
should any vital step be proposed to be taken, I beg you will
take the voice of Mr. Jameson also. And when Messrs. Troup
and Ward are here, pray admit them to your confidence, and
let them speak freely their opinions. I think I have written
very clearly upon everything that strikes me as necessary.
Your treatment of the natives, I suggest, should depend
entirely upon their conduct to you. Suffer them to return to
the neighbouring villages in peace, and if you can in any
manner, by moderation, small gifts occasionally of brass rods,
&c., hasten an amicable intercourse, I should recommend your
doing so. Lose no opportunity of obtaining all kinds of information respecting the natives, the position of the various
villages in your neighbourhood, &c., &c.

I have the honour to be, your obedient servant,

HENRY M. STANLEY,

Commanding Expedition.

Since Mr. Stanley's departure nothing had been heard of or
from Tippo Tib and his promised aid.

During the first three days after our arrival all hands were

busy arranging the stores and loading the steamer with wood
fuel for its return passage down the Congo. Late in the
afternoon of the third day we were surprised by the sound of
gunshots in a temporary native village on the opposite side of
the Aruimi River, and we soon recognised the white gowns and
turbans of the Arab's mercenaries engaged in their bloody
work of slave-catching. Upon perceiving the steamer and our
camp they disappeared, and when Bonny and I crossed the
river in a small native canoe to speak with them, we found that
they had all retired to the forest before we reached the shore.

The following day *Le Stanley* left Yambuya to return down
river, and soon afterwards Abdallah, an Arab half-caste, the
chief of the Arab's mercenaries who plundered the village on
the opposite side of the river, came into our camp and informed
us that he and his following were a portion of the party of
carriers promised by Tippo Tib to carry our loads, and that on
the journey to Yambuya from Tippo Tib's head-quarters at
Stanley Falls, they had been forced to disband on account of
native hostility. That small parties had been sent to find our
camp, and that Abdallah and his followers were one of these
search parties. He stated that Tippo Tib was perfectly willing
to supply us with the promised number of men, and as Stanley
Falls was only a few days' journey it might be advisable for an
officer to visit him personally, with a view to arranging for
the reorganisation of the promised contingent, and that he
(Abdallah) would act as guide to Stanley Falls. Jameson and
myself were instructed by Major Barttelot to proceed with

Abdallah to Tippo Tib, and make every effort to obtain the promised carriers as soon as possible.

To have marched from Yambuya in stages—as Mr. Stanley gave us the option of doing (failing the aid from Tippo Tib), in the clause, " Then it would be better to make two marches of six miles twice over, if you prefer marching to staying for our arrival "—with the bulk of the expedition stores and ammunition, through dense forest and undergrowth, with men who were utterly unreliable, men who had been so to speak " weeded out " both at Bolobo and Yambuya, when Mr. Stanley selected the 383 men for the Advance Column, men who for the most part were acknowledged bad characters, " weakest in body " and the invalids of the expedition : to have marched then, under these circumstances, without first exhausting every chance of obtaining the 600 carriers from Tippo Tib that were required to enable us to march altogether, would have rendered us blameable for disregarding the clause in Mr. Stanley's instructions :—" The loss of these men" (our garrison of Zanzibaris and Soudanese) " and goods would be certain ruin to us, and the Advance Force itself would need to solicit relief in its turn."

Tippo Tib promised to collect the men together at once, and assured us that in a few weeks at least we should receive the necessary men.

From that time the tragedy of the Rear Guard commenced. Tippo Tib continued to procrastinate, the Zanzibaris and Soudanese, unused to the food of the country, sickened and died. Each of the five officers was in turn stricken down at death's door with malarial fevers and dysentery. No news whatever reached Yambuya from the Advance Guard. Month after month of horrors passed, and still no aid was sent us by Tippo Tib, and we were soon rendered powerless to act in any way, on account of the emaciated condition of the Zanzibaris and Soudanese.

Mr. Stanley calculated that by November, five months from the date of his departure from Yambuya, he would return, but time passed on and still not a word was heard of or from him. In March 1888, four months after the time that Mr. Stanley was expected to return to Yambuya, Major Barttelot, by way of a final attempt to obtain the promised carriers from Tippo Tib, sent Mr. Jameson to Kassongo, Tippo Tib's principal stronghold, about a month's journey up the Congo above Stanley Falls, and in order to acquaint the Committee with the position of affairs, he instructed me to find my way to the West Coast and despatch the following message from the nearest cable station :—

Copy of Telegram.

No news of Stanley since writing last October.[1] Tippo Tib went Kassongo November sixteenth, but up to March has only got us two hundred and fifty men ; more are coming, but in uncertain numbers, and at uncertain times. Presuming Stanley in trouble, absurd for me to start with less numbers than he did, I carrying more loads, and minus " Maxim " gun ;

---

[1] Alluding to vague reports from deserters. No authentic news from Mr. Stanley ever reached Yambuya after his departure.

therefore have sent Jameson Kassongo to hasten Tippo in regard to remainder of originally promised six hundred men, and to obtain from him as many fighting men as possible up to four hundred; to make most advantageous terms he can as regards service and payment of men, he and I guaranteeing money in name of expedition. Jameson will return about May fourteenth, but earliest date to start will be June first. When I start, propose leaving officer with all loads not absolutely wanted at Stanley Falls. Ward carries this message. Please obtain wire from King Belgians to Administrator " Free State," to place carriers at his disposal, and have steamer in readiness to convey him Yambuya. If men come before his arrival, start without him. He should return about July first. Wire advice and opinion. Officers all well. Ward awaits reply.

BARTTELOT.

William Mackinnon (Gray, Dawes, & Co.),
  14 Austin Friars, London.

Leaving Yambuya on March 28, I hastened down the Congo River in two canoes, journeying night and day, and despatched the cable on May 1, after thirty-two days' incessant travelling, and received the following reply from the Committee :—

Major Bartlelot, care Ward, Congo.

Committee refer you to Stanley's orders of June 24, 1887. If you still cannot march in accordance with these orders, then stay where you are, awaiting his arrival, or until you receive fresh instructions from Stanley. Committee do not authorise engagement of fighting men. News has been received from Emin Pacha, *viâ* Zanzibar, dated Wadelai, November 2. Stanley was not then heard of. Emin Pacha is well, and is in no immediate want of supplies, and goes to south-west of lake to watch for Stanley. Letters have been posted regularly, *viâ* East Coast.

(Signed) CHAIRMAN OF COMMITTEE.

On my return journey up-country I received a letter from Major Barttelot instructing me to remain at Bangala (a State station on the Upper Congo, 1,000 miles from the coast), in charge of certain loads he had sent down to that station. It appears that during my absence Mr. Jameson returned to Yambuya from Kassongo with a sufficient number of men from Tippo Tib to enable them to march, and that Mr. J. Rose Troup had been invalided home, after having suffered intensely from a complicated illness produced by poverty of blood.

After remaining a few weeks at Bangala, news reached me of the assassination of Major Barttelot, and a few days afterwards Mr. Jameson reached Bangala in an unconscious condition, after descending the Congo from Stanley Falls, 500 miles, in canoes. On the following day after his arrival he died from the effects of bilious fever, produced by exposure and privation. After burying my poor comrade I set off again to the coast to cable the sad news of this fresh disaster to London, and in reply was instructed to return and collect the remainder of the expedition, and bring them down to the coast. While on the journey into the interior I heard of Mr. Stanley's return to the scene of Major Barttelot's assassination, and that he had taken Mr. Bonny and all that remained of the men and loads of the Rear Guard back with him to Emin Pacha's province.

Hoping for an opportunity of following Mr. Stanley, or at least of obtaining further news, I continued my journey to Stanley Falls, and, finding it was impossible to follow, and after remaining among the Arabs for upwards of a month and learning nothing further from Mr. Stanley, I returned with a few survivors, in addition to my own little band of Zanzibaris, and was instructed by the Committee to return home, as any further action on my part was impossible.

As a volunteer in the expedition I was not entitled to receive any pay for my services, but the Committee graciously granted me the sum of £330, together with the following letter :—

DEAR SIR,—I have the pleasure, by desire of the Emin Relief Committee, of sending you the following copy of a minute passed at their meeting to-day :—" The Committee wish to record their full appreciation of the services Mr. Ward has rendered to the expedition, and the faithful manner in which he has performed the duties entrusted to him."

I am, yours faithfully,

F. DE WINTON, *Hon. Sec.*

Emin Relief Committee, July 5, 1889.

Unfortunately, there are conflicting opinions upon the actions of the Rear Guard. No doubt Mr. Stanley suffered a great shock upon learning the sad tale of Yambuya with its hundred graves, but in "In Darkest Africa" he takes much too harsh a view of a portion of his expedition that endured great hardships while doing their best. Of the five officers, two lost their lives in his service, and a third contracted illnesses from which it is doubtful whether he will ever fully recover.

H. W.

LONDON: *September* 8, 1890.

The illustrations on pp. 112 and 115 are from photographs kindly given to me by Mr. Darby, the Baptist missionary of Lukolela.

Mr. W. J. Davy rendered me valuable aid by developing my photographic negatives.

PART I.
LOWER CONGO.

FIVE YEARS

WITH THE

CONGO CANNIBALS.

CHAPTER I.

INTRODUCTORY.

BOYHOOD—SAILING FOR NEW ZEALAND—SEVEN YEARS ROUGHING IT—VOYAGE ROUND THE
HORN—BORNEO—DEATH OF FRANK HATTON—RETURN TO ENGLAND—JOSEPH HATTON.

AN irresistible desire to see the great world, to wander through
strange countries, and to associate with barbarians who dwell
far from the jostling and hurrying of civilization, prompted
me to leave my English home at the age of fifteen, and to seek
incident in a roving life away from my own kith and kin.

When I acknowledge that the only prize I ever gained at
school was a pocket telescope awarded me by the committee of
athletic sports for my acrobatic performance upon the horizontal
bar; when I state that my literary taste was confined to records
of travel and adventure, and that I eagerly read every book upon
these subjects from Herodotus to Robinson Crusoe—in whom,
by the way, I took a deep personal interest—further comment
upon my boyhood is needless.

When I made known my determination to set out into the

world, my parents emphatically shook their heads. A few of my relatives whose interest in my welfare had only hitherto taken the form of a trifling monetary present upon the occasion of my birthday, grew enthusiastic in their denunciations of me, and were profuse in their prophecies that I would become a worthless vagabond. My father informed me that I was to be disinherited, and, when interviewing his lawyer with this object, I can vividly recall my indignant feelings on hearing the legal gentleman remark in an undertone : "Well, Mr. Ward, if he was a son of mine, I would soon change his views with a horsewhip."

One wintry morning shortly after this, in a typical London fog, amid the gruff voices of half drunken sailors busy hauling ropes and heaving capstan bars, the English barque, "James Wishart," was extricated from the maze of docks, and I, with my hands deep down in my otherwise empty pockets, formed one of the little group of poor emigrants who were huddled together on the main deck.

We were bound for Auckland, New Zealand, but from the sad expression upon the tearful and unwashed faces of some of my fellow voyagers, a casual observer might have inferred that we were bound for a much more inhospitable land.

It was in this way that my life of travel and adventure commenced, and I faced the world a friendless boy with a stout heart and strong arms as my only capital.

I was willing to turn my hand to anything, and during the four years that I remained in New Zealand and Australia my occupations were so many and so various, that, looking back on this portion of my career, I am surprised at my own versatility. I was by turns a stock-rider, a circus performer, and a miner. I never knew what character changing circumstances might compel me to assume, or to what industry I should be indebted for my daily bread. I am afraid that my ability in my different callings might have been measured by the supply of this necessary article—which was oftentimes small enough.

It was a rough but wholesome apprenticeship that I served. If I lacked the advantages of friends and influence, I at least learned early in life to depend on my own resources, and was able to prevent myself being trodden underfoot in this hurrying, selfish, overcrowded world.

Four years of rough life and hard work, with alternations of small successes and many reverses, passed, and I determined, as an opportunity offered, to return to my own home. I shipped as an able-bodied seaman on board a sailing ship bound for England *via* San Francisco. Perhaps the most trying of all my experiences was that never to be-forgotten voyage, with its fearful, weary mid-winter passage around the stormy Horn. Seven weeks were we rounding the Cape, and it was seven months after leaving San Francisco that I sailed into Plymouth, after having thus worked my way round the world.

A brief stay in England and I was away again, this time bound for Borneo as a cadet in the service of the British North Borneo Company, which had recently received its royal charter. On arrival in Borneo I was appointed to a station in the far interior of that wild and almost unknown country. There for seven months I lived, surrounded by tribes of Dyak head hunters, and there also I contracted malarial fever, which threatened to put an end to all my wanderings and adventures. My life was for some time despaired of, recovery was out of the question in the fever-stricken jungles of the island, and I was placed on board a coasting steamer bound for Chinese ports, and whose voyage eventually took me to Japan. But this expedient was of little avail in my case, for the fever had so firm a hold on me that I felt that I should be unable to free myself from its grip while in the East, so once more I turned my face homewards.

If my Borneo experiences were rendered unsatisfactory through ill-health, it is to this portion of my life that I am indebted for a friendship which has in many ways influenced my later life. It happened that one day while at my solitary station, news was brought to me by a Malay that a white man had accidentally shot himself at some distance from where I then was. It was my poor friend Frank Hatton, from whom I had parted but a few days before, whose life of much achievement and more promise was ended in this tragic manner. Whilst tracking an elephant through the forest, his gun became entangled in a creeper, the trigger caught and the charge entered his right lung, killing him almost instantly. I had become much attached to Frank Hatton during the short time we had spent together, and my first thought on my return, when renewed health enabled me to get about, was to seek out his father.

Mr. Joseph Hatton was then in America with Mr. Henry Irving, and hearing that some one had arrived from Borneo who could supplement the meager details of the catastrophe he was then in possession of, he hastened his return to England, and immediately on his arrival home sought me out to hear all that I could tell him of the cruel circumstances that deprived him of an only and dearly loved son.

It was through Mr. Hatton that I procured an interview with Mr. Henry M. Stanley, and thus, by a chain of circumstances, an event happening in a far away Eastern island was the means of sending me to the heart of Central Africa.

So strange are the influences at work in shaping our fortunes, that the disaster which made me a messenger of ill tidings to England is in a way connected with the writing of this book, and as I jot down to-day my reminiscences of five years' life with the Congo cannibals, it seems that I can almost hear the report of the fatal shot echoing through the Bornean forest.

CHAPTER II.

INTERVIEW WITH H. M. STANLEY—SERVICES ACCEPTED—CONTRACT—LANDING AT THE MOUTH OF THE CONGO—TRANSPORT SERVICE—APPOINTED TO BANGALA—PATHETIC LANDMARKS.

I SHALL always remember my first interview with Mr. Stanley, which took place at his rooms in Sackville street, London. Mr. Stanley had then just completed his work of creating the Congo Free State, which the following year received the recognition of all the Great Powers at the Berlin conference and was placed under the sovereignty of His Majesty King Leopold II. of the Belgians. The room in which I was received impressed me as characteristic of the man. There were here no ornaments or bric-à-brac, nor were the walls hung with the guns and trophies of the explorer. Everything spoke of earnest, tireless work; floor and tables bore traces of it, littered as they were with manuscripts, maps, and scattered papers and pamphlets, while amid the confusion everywhere around I detected the famous Congo cap, which has figured in so many illustrations, thrown carelessly on a sideboard.

My reception was kindly and gravely courteous, but there was a solemnity in Mr. Stanley's manner that hardly at first put me at my ease. I felt at the time that I was being analyzed and summarized by those searching gray eyes, and the impassive expression of the countenance gave me no indication of what the verdict might be.

The few questions Mr. Stanley addressed to me seemed framed

for the purpose of discovering what my real object was in asking to be sent to Central Africa.

He told me he had heard of me through Mr. Hatton, and understood that I wished to try my fortunes in the great country that he had opened up.

To test me he spoke discouragingly of the climate of Equatorial Africa.

"People die there," said he, solemnly.

I muttered something about Borneo and fever. He looked amused for a moment, and then said :

"Well, after all, the Congo is a sanitorium compared to Borneo. You seem suited for the life," he continued, when I told him how I had already "roughed it" in different parts of the globe. "If, however, I decide to send you, I should of course require some testimonials, as abroad you would occupy positions of great trust and responsibility."

This was a very natural request, but somehow I had not anticipated it, and was for the moment rather nonplussed, until a happy thought struck me, and taking from my pocket my sailor's discharges, I handed them to him.

He seemed at once pleased and satisfied as he examined my humble credentials, and I could not help thinking that the little scrap of crumpled paper which records the conduct and ability of poor "Jack," might have awakened reminiscences of a time when he too had sustained life "before the mast" on salt pork and weather-beaten biscuit.

In a few days I received word that my services were accepted and that I was to proceed to the Congo in a steamer leaving Liverpool two weeks from that time.

The envelope containing this intimation also contained two

documents, both equally remarkable in their way. One was the contract of services, and the other a list of articles considered essential to the outfit for an officer in the Congo Free State.

It was the first attempt made by the Belgians at colonization, and both official papers showed a plentiful lack of knowledge, and an earnest effort to cloak this apparent defect with a wealth of imaginative clauses and details. The list of clothes recommended by the sapient board of Belgian generals and colonels who had charge of this department, fairly bristled with humorous suggestions. The necessity of providing myself with an alpenstock was impressed on me with utmost gravity, and I was urged with all the weight of governmental authority not to start on the voyage without providing myself with two pairs of trousers, one cork helmet and a jackknife.

As no force could be brought to bear to compel me to supply myself with these articles, which I was left at liberty to purchase with my own money, I was able to enjoy a laugh over the absurdities of this extraordinary list.

But the contract was another matter, and its clauses, ridiculous and childish as they were, were calculated to annoy rather than to amuse. I was warned that if at any time I fell ill, I must do so at my own risk and expense, and it was almost implied that if I died while in the service of the State, such conduct would be considered most reprehensible. There were other clauses forbidding me to write or publish anything in connection with the Congo, and there were forfeits and penalties to be exacted for any independent action on my part. In fact the whole was so constructed that those who for a miserable pittance volunteered service in a deadly climate, received little or no consideration in return for the risks they ran. Yet so anxious was I to commence my new career that I signed a recognition of these innumerable restrictions, in a contract which was to extend over a period of three years.

I landed at the mouth of the Congo in October, 1884, and proceeded immediately to Vivi, a station at the commencement of the cataract region, which was at that time the principal depot on the river. Sir Francis de Winton, who had been appointed administrator after Mr. Stanley's departure in the spring of the year, made his headquarters here, and on reporting myself to him I was appointed to the manual transport service of the Lower Congo, whose business it was to secure native porters for the carriage of loads to stations in the interior. After fifteen months of this work, during which time I traveled considerably among the Bakongo tribes, I was appointed to command the station of the Bangalas, which was the most thickly populated district in the Congo State. Here I remained for six months, until the arrival of a new administrator, General (Mons.) Jaunsens, whose policy it was to replace English pioneers by Belgian military officers, and who, in a letter profuse of compliments, informed me that on account of my knowledge of the Kikongo language, my services were indispensable in the transport service of the cataract region, relieved me of my command, and replaced me by one of his own countrymen. The whole service was reorganized by the new administrator, and great changes took place in the *personnel* of the State service. In the early days the pioneers had been selected from every nationality, but those who had borne the hardships of the early days were now either shelved or forced to seek service elsewhere. The majority of these early pioneers had a history. They generally came out to the Congo with good health, enthusiasm, and brand new kits. Their strange doings during the commencement of their African careers often supplied material for humorous anecdotes. The end was more frequently pathetic.

One may sometimes stumble upon an ant-eaten wooden cross, and a little heap of rough stones hidden away in the high grass and brambles. This is the resting-place of some proud young fellow stricken down in early manhood. One cannot tell, perhaps, who it is who lies there, for many men have come and gone since then, and it is more than probable that the friend who formed this rude grave has been himself laid away in another part of the country. How many sorrowing mothers, wives and sweethearts grieve for the loved ones laid low by the deadly fever of Congo land. How they try and picture to themselves what the dread country is like. A mighty river, dusky savages and graceful palms, all lit up with a fierce tropical sun, probably figure most in their fancies; and then the sacred little budget of letters from the loved one in the interior of Africa with "Stamps not procurable" written on the envelopes, which bear curious postmarks. Then they are carefully tied together, handled with loving care and heartrending sadness, written with faded, diluted ink on different sized sheets of paper, full of long, puzzling native names of places, erratic sentences, and allusions to unknown persons and events, for the fevered brain is apt to wander, and seldom do letters connect events, for often a letter will be lost on the overland march down country, and consequently the thread of connecting news is broken—pages full of expectancy of the return home—heaps of questions about family and friends, that, alas, remain forever unanswered. Then comes a formal official intimation, in a large blue envelope, from Brussels, couched in cold, polite phrases of condolence. The loved one will return no more. Months ago the body was laid away in the ground under the shade of palms. No noise will disturb the endless sleep, for a cry of a passing bird, or at night the hoarse croaking of frogs in the swamps near by, is the only sound that breaks in on the silence and seclusion of this sacred spot.

CHAPTER III.

The Kikongo language—Travels among the Bakongo—News of the Emin Pasha Expedition—Meeting Stanley—A picturesque procession—I join the expedition—Left in charge at Bolobo—The rear guard.

IN the summer of 1886, I found myself at my old post in the transport service on the Lower Congo, and from that time until the early part of 1887, I continued traveling hither and thither in my quest for native carriers, and, as by hard study I had become proficient in the Kikongo language, I was able to note many curious customs and quaint superstitions current in the little known villages of the Bakongo. My note-book and sketch-book were always at hand during these wanderings, and besides affording me the keenest pleasure, the rough notes with which I filled them gave a permanency to impressions that would otherwise in the course of time have faded from my memory.

I had now spent two years and a half in Central Africa, and although the life exercised a strong fascination over me, I felt at times a longing for glimpses of the outside world other than those afforded me by newspapers whose latest intelligence was six months old, and I was journeying down to the coast with the intention of boarding the first homeward-bound steamer, when the news reached me at Matadi of the expedition for the relief of Emin Pacha, and of Stanley's expected return in command. This changed all my plans, and the enthusiasm I had felt at the prospect of returning to my own country died away, and my sole hope and desire now was to be enlisted in the little band who were bound for far regions in Equatorial Africa, to carry relief to a brave and devoted man. Hastening back to Lukunga with Charles Ingham, who had been sent by Stanley to make arrangements for the transport of his load, I assisted him in engaging several hundred native carriers for the work, and a few days afterwards I was leading about four hundred Bakongo down country by forced marches. I had broken camp early one morning, and was marching rapidly along ahead of my caravan, when in the distance, coming over the brow of a hill, I saw a tall Soudanese soldier bearing Gordon Bennett's yacht flag. Behind him and astride of a fine henna-stained mule, whose silver-plated trappings shone in the bright morning sun, was Mr. Henry M. Stanley, attired in his famous African costume. Following immediately in his rear were his personal servants, Somalis with their curious braided waistcoats and white robes; then came Zanzibaris with their blankets, water bottles, ammunition belts and guns; stalwart Soudanese soldiery with dark hooded coats, their rifles on their backs, and innumerable straps and leather belts around their bodies, Zanzibari porters bearing iron-bound boxes of ammunition, to which were fastened axes and shovels, as well as their little bundles of clothing, which were rolled up in coarse, sandy-colored blankets.

Stanley saluted me very cordially and dismounted. "Take a seat," said he, with a wave of his hand indicating the bare ground. We then squatted down and he handed me a cigar from the silver case given him by H. R. H. the Prince of Wales, on the night before his departure.

As concisely as possible I told him of my desire to join his expedition, and after a few minutes' conversation Mr. Stanley said that he would accept me as a volunteer. He then expressed his surprise at my healthy appearance, considering that I had been so long in Africa. Having directed me to hurry on with my natives to Matadi, to bring up the loads, and as expeditiously as possible

HENRY M. STANLEY.

overtake him at Stanley Pool, where we should all embark together, we parted.

Passing along I became further acquainted with the constitution of Stanley's great cavalcade. At one point a steel whale boat was being carried in sections, suspended from poles which were

each borne by four men ; donkeys heavily laden with sacks of rice
were next met with, and a little further on the women of Tippo
Tib's harem, their faces partly concealed and their bodies draped
in gaudily colored cotton cloths ; then at intervals along the line
of march an English officer, with whom, of course, I exchanged
friendly salutations ; then several large-horned East African goats
driven by saucy little Zanzibari boys. A short distance further
on an abrupt turn of the narrow foot-path brought into view
the dignified form of the renowned Tippo Tib, as he strolled along
majestically in his flowing Arab robes of dazzling whiteness, and
carrying over his left shoulder a richly decorated sabre, which was
an emblem of office conferred on him by H. H. the Sultan of
Zanzibar. Behind him at a respectful distance followed several
Arab sheiks, whose bearing was quiet and dignified. In response
to my salutation they bowed most gracefully.

"Haijambo," said I.

"Sijambo," they replied.

"Khabari gani ?" (what news,) I enquired.

"Khabari njema," (good news,) was the reply, and in that way
I passed along the line of 700 men, in whose ranks were represented various types from all parts of Eastern Equatorial Africa,
each wearing the distinguishing garb of his own country. All the
costumes and accoutrements looked bright and gay, for the expedition had disembarked but a few days previously. As the
procession filed along the narrow, rugged path, it produced an
effect no less brilliant than striking. Its unbroken line extended
over a distance of probably four miles.

The transport work concluded, I rejoined the expedition at
Stanley Pool, where we embarked in three light-draughted river
steamers for the journey on the Upper Congo.

At Bolobo the first post of the expedition was formed and left in my charge, the body of the expedition then proceeding up river to the rapids of the Aruimi, where the intrenched camp of the Rear Guard was established. It was to this column, under the command of the late Major Barttelot, that I was attached. The tragic events which befell the members of the ill-fated Rear Guard are already sufficiently familiar to the public, and have no refer- ence to the subject matter of this book, which contains the records of my own observations of the domestic life and character of the Congo savages during a period of five years.

CHAPTER IV.

THE BAKONGO – THEIR VILLAGES — KING OF CONGO — NGANGA NKISSI — TRIAL FOR WITCH-CRAFT — NKASA POISON — DEATH OF NKOBA — "THE WILL OF THE GREAT SPIRIT" — ACQUITTED.

THE Bakongo tribes, inhabiting the cataract region of the Lower Congo, are a mild-tempered and unwarlike race in comparison with the savages of the interior. Cannibalism is unknown among them, and they shudder with repugnance at the mere mention of eating human flesh.

They are a tall, gracefully formed race, with pleasing features, only slightly disfigured by tribal marks, and the teeth are, as a rule, left to adorn the mouth in their natural shapes, and are not filed into points as are those of so many of the Upper Congo tribes.

The villages of the Bakongo are generally situated on hill-tops— few are at the edge of the river—and are surrounded by thick groves of trees, among which the palm is ever conspicuous. In addition to the juice it yields to the incisions of the natives, known as *malafu*, the palm tree also supplies them with food in the shape of palm-nuts, the oily covering of which is used in cooking and in flavoring their dishes of vegetables—sweet-potatoes, beans, cabbage or manioc-tops—the hard nut is cracked and the white kernel eaten ; and the fronds of the palm tree supply material for building their houses, while the leaves are often used as roofing in lieu of the grass which is the common covering of all houses in the Bakongo country.

c

Their villages are small in size—a score or so of huts clustered together ; few contain five hundred people, if indeed any one village may be said to possess that number, but then, as every hilltop in some parts of the country is covered with grass huts, the population spreading throughout the area is great.

Each village exists under the separate government of its own chief or head man, who recognizes no superior, although at one time the entire country for hundreds of miles owned the sway of the potentate, styling himself the King of Congo, who had his capital at San Salvador, a small village at the present day situated in the Portuguese dominions, some eighty miles south of the Congo River, and probably one hundred and fifty miles from the seacoast.   There is still a " King of Congo," self-styled, living at San Salvador, Dom Pedro V. ; but his authority is only nominal over the villages in the immediate vicinity of his capital, and the natives beyond that radius, although they speak of him as the *Ntotila*, a title equivalent to head king or emperor, owe no allegiance to Dom Pedro, or, if owing it, make no pretense of discharging its obligations.

The chiefs of the different villages exercise much authority ; and, in public affairs, the waging of war against a neighbor, or the concluding of peace after hostilities, their opinion is generally supreme in the council of headmen who debate these matters. But it is the *nganga nkissi*, the charm-doctor, who sways the minds and lives of men, and possesses a power superior to that of the chiefs, in that these also are bound by the same bonds of superstition as the people.   Every village has its *nganga nkissi*, and the superstitious dread in which the people hold him, by reason of the supernatural power he is credited with possessing, owing to his supposed secret understanding with the spirit-world, enables him to largely influence the decision of all affairs of public importance, as well as to be supreme in those of a domestic nature.

It is a general belief with the Bakongo that all sickness is the result of witchcraft exercised by some member of the community, and the services of the charm-doctor are employed to discover the individual who is *ndoki*, *i. e.* bedeviled, and guilty of devouring the spirit of the unfortunate invalid ; and in the event of the sick person dying, the medicine-man is deputed by the relatives of the deceased to find out the witch who has "eaten the heart." They believe the spirit (*moyo*) is situated in the middle of the heart, and it is regarded as the mainspring of all human actions, the inspirer of good and bad deeds alike ; so that to bewitch the spirit in a man's heart is to cause him to waste away and die.

Upon these occasions, the charm-doctor comes with his elaborate apparatus of charms, consisting of fish-bones, snake-heads, wild cats' skins, egg-shells, and a supply of powdered chalk.

Seating himself, he cleverly manipulates his charms, and performs a series of sleight-of-hand tricks. The grass mat that he sits upon seems to be endowed with life, and the crafty impostor affects astonishment, and, shrugging his shoulders, he shakes his head as though the affair was quite beyond his control. At intervals, he bends down and listens with his head on the earth; then he will bound into the air and execute a variety of frantic gesticulations, clutching with open hands as though trying to catch some invisible being. Then he gazes intently upon the various persons around him, who are all more or less silent and breathless in awe. Usually before declaring the name of the poor wretch whom he accuses of being *ndoki* (possessed of the Evil Spirit), he demands payment for his services from the relatives of the dead person, and in this transaction he shows that his connection with the spiritual world by no means lessens his shrewdness in looking after his own interests, and he is not easily imposed upon, either as regards the quantity or quality of the remuneration he demands for his fantastic services.

The unfortunate victim selected by the charm-doctor as being *ndoki* has to undergo the poison ordeal to prove his or her guilt or innocence. A decoction is made from the poisonous bark of a tree known as *nkasa*. It is usually administered at sunrise. During the day the victim is tormented by the jeers and insults of all the people of the tribe, who, half intoxicated, dance around him, and do everything in their power to worry the wretched victim. If by sunset the *nkasa* poison should act as an emetic, then the innocence of the accused is demonstrated and the victim is released, but, on the other hand, should the dose prove fatal, then the justice of the ordeal is fairly established, and they are satisfied that they have in this way killed the evil power, and the accusation of witchcraft is considered to have been brought home to the right person.

The regard in which the *nganga* is held does not prevent him sometimes from accepting bribes either from the relations of a man lately dead, who suggest, when giving this engagement "retainer," that So-and-so is, in their opinion, the guilty person, or from the poor wretch who has been named as *ndoki* to secure the good offices of the *nganga* in brewing the *nkasa* draught ; for many of them shrewdly believe that although their innocence may be good defense enough, still it is just as well to have the *nganga* in a friendly mood, so that the *nkasa* may not be *too* strong.

Whatever the notion that impels them to make presents to

THE ANTICS OF THE CHARM DOCTOR

the *nganga* may be, he certainly grows rich, sleek and fat on these gifts.

The first instance that came under my notice of the power of the *nganga nkissi* occurred shortly after my arrival in the Bakongo country.

During a hunting expedition, a somewhat influential chief named Nkoba was overtaken by a wounded female elephant, who, lifting him from the ground with her trunk, impaled him on one of her tusks. The poor fellow lived but a few hours, as mortification set in.

Terrible was the wailing of his adherents, who fired guns continually day and night, until their powder was finished. His property, which consisted of a few china cups and four colored umbrellas, was hung about the house in which he was laid in state, while his six wives watched and wailed around the body. All his followers shaved their heads in token of mourning, and the whole district was assembled before the *nganga nkissi*, who was to pronounce whether the elephant was possessed of the devil or had been bewitched by some enemy of the dead chief, or whether it was a case of *Diambudi-nzambi*, the will of the Great Spirit.

It was about an hour before sundown, when all were seated, anxiously expectant to hear the decision of the medicine-man. There were upward of five hundred present, ranged in a hollow square about thirty deep. Dead silence ranged as the *nganga* leaped into their midst, rattling in his hands images, leopard-claws and calabash-tops, and chanted a weird song, the chorus of which was taken up by all present, to an accompaniment of drums and clapping of hands. At times the chorus rose to such a pitch that the air seemed to vibrate, whilst the next moment the excited singers hushed their song to a low, humming murmur. After reciting all the facts of the case with a drawling intonation, he executed a dance, the like of which I had never seen before. The wild, leaping figure, with its dress of leopard skins and charms, presented a weird picture. As the sun went down, and darkness crept over the surrounding scene and fell on the eager assembly, excitement rose to its highest pitch, as the *nganga* proclaimed in a loud and solemn tone, that Nkoba's death was the will of the Great Spirit, *Diambu di-nzambi*, and that no evil influence had been at work in the matter.

I may add that I afterward ascertained from my followers that my presence had influenced the *nganga's* finding, for if he had pronounced otherwise, some victim would have been selected to drink the *nkasa* poison, and this he knew I would use every means in my power to prevent.

CHAPTER V.

CASES of suicide occasionally occur among the Bakongo, al-though much less frequently than in civilized communities.
With them, the cause is attributed to anger, that being an emotion they feel very powerfully.

A native will get angry with his relatives, angry with himself ; things will not go with him as they should, he thinks, and so one day, in a fit of rage, he kills himself, and his friends remark that poor Sakala or Kokisa got angry (*lou*) and made away with him-self.

Inland from the river and away from the frequented caravan route, the people are notable for natural eloquence, which the many soft inflections of their language and the harmonious euphony of its concording syllables enable them to freely indulge in.

Their language is particularly rich in expression and soft in sound, the words being composed principally of vowels; l's, m's and n's are the predominating consonants. The plural of substan-tives is formed by prefixes, and an alliterative concord is one of the principal features of the language, which is classed as a branch of the African Bantu tongue. The Zulu language is also consid-ered by philologists to be a branch of this so-called Bantu tongue, which appears to be the root of nearly all the many dialects spoken by the varied and numerous tribes south of the equator.

Although the vocabularies of the different tribes in the Congo country differ widely, yet the construction of their language is more or less the same, and after mastering the language of one tribe, one can more readily acquire a knowledge of the dialect spoken by a neighbouring tribe.

" Palavers," or public discussions, are dear to the heart of all Africans, and a very trivial cause may give rise to a great flow of talk among the Bakongo. They reason well and are born debaters, but should a native consider himself weaker in argumentative powers than his opponent, he will hire an advocate.

A native at a palaver always holds in his left hand a number of small pieces of split bamboo, or other small sticks, and he caps each point of his argument by placing one of these on the ground before him. By the time he has stated all the leading facts and the main points of his story, there will be a long line of these little pieces of wood arranged in front of him, and if he should have occasion to refer to any past matter of his speech, he will pick up the stick having reference to that subject and lay it down again in its place when he has exhausted the theme.

Some speaker on the opposition side of the circle will object, probably, to our friend's allusion to that question—which may be in reference to Kiukela's pig, or Mbatchi's fowl which Luemba stole, or was accused of stealing—and when the stick having reference to the fowl is lifted, he will step in, exclaiming : " No, no ; not that one," and may seize another stick, dealing with a totally different part of the discussion—how the speaker's own cousin walked off with Luemba's string of broiled rats or lumps of sugar cane, last market day—and try to get up a counter charge against him, until the sticks of pig and fowl, and of rats and sugar cane, get hopelessly muddled up, and a loud murmur of indignation from the friends of number one forces number two to retreat to his own side, and leave the unfortunate orator to endeavor to arrange his bamboo sticks in their proper order, and put the pig and fowl back into their places in the forefront of his narration. He may possibly avenge himself for this interruption by going over the whole story again from the very beginning, which dates from the very earliest times, and refers to the remote ancestors of Luemba and Mbatchi. This is truly a refinement of oratorical cruelty ; and were it not that his opponents are able ultimately to re-inflict the whole tale, with compound interest, referring to this very interruption and his reply, again on him, they could not undergo the ordeal and support life.

In answering questions, the Bakongo will generally try and tell the questioner what they think will please him most, quite ignoring the truthfulness we consider it necessary to observe in our replies.

The Bakongo are a mild and inoffensive race ; they have few vices, and their virtues are of a negative order. They share largely the two principal characteristics of the African ; superstition and selfishness. Evidences of gratitude are rare indeed, although occasionally one meets with this sentiment in odd guises. Once, by a happy chance, I saved a baby's life. The child was brought to me by its mother in convulsions, and I was fortunate enough to find in my medicine chest a drug that effected an almost immediate cure. Yet the service I rendered to this woman, instead of meeting with any appreciation, only procured for me the whispered reputation of being a witch. This and many other instances of a like nature caused me to reflect somewhat bitterly on the lack of kindliness in the native character.

Returning to this district after an absence of many months, I camped one night near the village where I had cured the child.

WOMAN OF THE BAKONGO.

About midnight I was disturbed by a woman's voice. The flickering light of the smouldering campfires threw the reflection of her figure on the flaps of my tent, as, thrusting her head and arm through the opening, she said in a hurried whisper:

"*Ma 'ma, oh Mayala Mbemba tambula diaki di'nsusu.*" (Here, here, Eagle's Wings, take this fowl's egg.)

Not clearly understanding the reason of this strange visit in the dark, I expostulated with the woman, and said:

"It is midnight; all the people are sleeping. I do not purchase food at midnight. Come at sunrise, and I will buy."

"No! do! I do not want to sell this egg; I give it to you. Do you forget that twenty moons ago you gave *dilonga* (a cure) to my sick baby. Mwan'ami now runs and plays in good health. You put fresh life into my baby. I want to give you payment. I am poor, but, here, take this fowl's egg. I come in the darkness that my people may not know, for they would jeer at me if they knew of this gift."

With mingled feelings of astonishment and sympathy for the poor woman, I placed the egg in one of my boots for safe keeping. I rolled up in my blanket, and was soon asleep again.

The next morning I handed the egg to my servant, instructing him how to poach it for my breakfast; and while waiting for my carriers to strike the tent and prepare their loads for the day's march, I took out my note-book and recorded the dialogue of the preceding night, and felt that I had been unjust in my judgment when, two years ago, I had considered that they were thankless and ungrateful. Whilst still writing, I was interrupted by my servant, who, holding in his dirty hands a broken egg-shell, said:

" Master, that egg was bad!"

The Babwende, a tribe living on the north bank of the Congo, opposite Manyanga, and stretching from that point up to the Kwilu on the north and to nearly Stanley Pool on the east, are a branch of the Bakongo, speaking a different dialect of the same language, or rather, pronouncing the same language in a different way.

They are probably the most superstitious and at the same time the most savage of the Bakongo tribes. Many of the men wear a couple of dogs' teeth, long, curved fangs, in a slit in the nose. They pierce the division between the nostrils, and then insert the teeth in the apertures, fastening the two roots together in the hole, and leaving the bare white points to protrude from each nostril in a way that resembles somewhat the tusks of a boar.

The Babwende are a strong, hardy race. Their backs and abdomens are profusely decorated with incisions in the flesh, that take the form of chains and winding cords that encircle the body, or often of crocodiles, or some wild beast. Those living near the Congo are expert fishermen, piloting their small canoes through the rapid and dangerous channels of the river in that part of its course, with great skill and bravery.

BABWENDE IDOLS.

So strongly are they imbued with faith in their charms that these fishermen will enter the Congo in places known to swarm with crocodiles and swim out to their fishing stakes to untie their nets, regardless of danger and relying solely upon the power of their charms to protect them from the voracious creatures which are ever on the lookout for victims. These amulets or charms consist of some collection of rubbish, which has been gathered by the *nganga*, tied up in a bag or a piece of antelope skin, blessed, and handed over to the confiding purchaser as an infallible safeguard against crocodiles.

The Babwende have a curious manner of sealing a bargain. The left hand opened out flat is passed across the open mouth, and the air is ejected with a slight hissing sound during the passage of the hand.

"The sleeping sickness," by some considered to be a form of *beri-beri*, is very prevalent among the Babwende and other Bakongo tribes. The sufferer is at first afflicted with a pain in the back of the neck, which gradually extends to the limbs, and an increased desire to sleep takes possession of him. This last feeling slowly becomes stronger and stronger, until at length he sleeps almost continuously, at any hour of the day or in any posture, or while engaged eating his midday meal he will fall into a stupid, heavy slumber. I have seen carriers, who were suffering from the early stages of sleeping-sickness, who would fall asleep while walking, and, when startled by a sudden shock, would slowly become aware of their surroundings, and regard their companions with a dull, dazed stare.

The end of this disease is always fatal; no cure has yet been discovered for it, nor do European doctors, who have treated some cases, know the causes or real nature of the malady. Sometimes it ravages whole districts among the Bakongo, and entire villages have been swept away by it.

This sickness is prevalent throughout the whole of the Congo basin, and is known to different tribes by different names. On the upper river it is called *ntolo*, and the direst curse a native can call down on an adversary is to express a wish that he may be "Waka ntolo" (struck with sleep).

There is an old tradition among the natives of Lutete, a district near Stanley Pool, that far away in the interior dwell a race of dwarfs, whose heads are so big and heavy that when they fall down, they cannot get up again without assistance !

Another of their beliefs is that to the southeast of Stanley Pool there is a tribe which feeds on dead bodies. They call this people the Avumbi, from "*vumbi*," the Kikongo for "corpse;" and although I never met a person who admitted having been among the Avumbi, the name and the story are commonly repeated.

CHAPTER VI.

NGALYIEMA'S GOAT—A MAN'S SPIRIT IN THE BRANCH OF A TREE—THE NKIMBA, A MASONIC
ORDER—MYSTERIOUS LANGUAGE—KING OF LIFE AND DEATH—BARBAROUS CUSTOMS—.
A WEEK OF FOUR DAYS—PORK HIGHLY ESTEEMED—A HUMAN SLAVE BARTERED FOR A
FAT HOG.

IN the year 1880, two English missionaries, who had but recently
established themselves at San Salvador, the *Congo dia Ntotila*
(Congo of the King) of the natives endeavored to obtain news
of Stanley Pool, and information concerning the road to it from
the villagers. In order to test the accuracy of the replies given
them, and to find out if the natives really had been there, they
asked repeatedly if any of them had seen the strange big East
African goat which Stanley had given to Ngalyiema, the chief of
Kintamo on the Pool, when he descended the Congo in 1877. All
their inquiries, however, produced no admission of having seen the
goat at the Pool, for the people were then full of distrust of the
white men and their object in asking this question.

Some years afterward, the missionaries discovered that the
reason they could obtain no reply to their inquiry was that the
people all thought that they, the missionaries, believed the goat
contained the spirit of the king of San Salvador, and therefore
they wished to obtain possession of it, and so exercise an evil
power over the king.

A peculiar superstition exists with respect to diseases of long
standing. In these cases, the *moyo* (spirit) of the sick man is supposed to have left his body and to be wandering at large, and the
aid of the charm-doctor is called in, to capture the wandering

D

spirit and bring it back to the body of the invalid. Generally, after a variety of complicated dances, the charm-doctor declares that he has successfully chased the wandering spirit into the branch of some tree. All the people of the town thereupon accompany the *nganga* to the indicated tree, and the strongest men are selected to break off the branch containing the sick man's spirit and carry it back to the town. On the road, they insinuate by their gestures, that the burden is a heavy one, and difficult to carry. When the branch is taken to the sick man's hut, he is placed in an upright position by its side ; the *nganga* chants and manipulates his charms, and the process of *vutulanga moyo*, or giving back the spirit, is supposed to have been completely effected.

Principally among the Bakongo tribes exists the ceremony of the *Nkimba*, a Masonic order, entitling the initiated to certain privileges over *mungwata* or the uninitiated. All the lads of ten or twelve years of age are eligible, and the majority of them pass through the educational course, which lasts from six months to two years, according to the tribal custom ; during all this time they are not permitted to wash themselves. They smother their bodies with various colored chalks and wear a costume made of grass, as illustrated in the accompanying drawing.

The women and children of the towns are in continual fear of the *Nkimba*, who are allowed to parade through the villages at any time of the day or night. Any article of food or clothing required by them can be appropriated without question if only the things belong to a *mungwata*, or uninitiated person.

At the induction ceremony, the candidate is required to drink a certain potion which renders him insensible. He is then declared to be dead, and is carried into the forests, where the opera-

tion of circumcision is performed. After awhile he is restored, and by the simple village folk he is believed to have been raised from the dead. He then receives a new name, and he professes not to be able to remember his former tribe or even his parents. The *Nkimba* declare the rainbow is their father, which they say appears in the heavens upon each occasion of the enrollment of a brother initiate. They also adopt a new language, which is of a mysterious character, and though taught to the males, is never disclosed to the females. It is possible that it is some old or archaic form of the Bantu tongue, conserved for religious purposes like the Sanskrit, the old Sclav and the Latin, or it may be nothing more than an arbitrary transmogrification of words such as are found in such artificial tongues as the Kinyume of Zanzibar.

Among the principal superstitions of the Bakongo is the belief that certain people have power over the elements ; this power is called *simbanga dizulu* (holding the heavens), and they frequently kidnap suspected people, keeping them close prisoners in time of drought, until the rain falls.

In many districts of the Bakongo tribes, there is a chief who is known as the King of Life and Death. He pronounces the death sentence upon murderers and malefactors, who are then barbarously executed in the market places.

A hole is dug in which the victim is placed in a standing position and buried up to the neck. A strong man then dashes out the poor wretch's brains with a huge stone, and earth is shovelled into a mound over the grave. Most market places are conspicuous by the numbers of such mounds of earth, which are always significant tokens of the fate of evil-doers.

Frequently, in the event of a person being afflicted with a malady considered by the authorities of the village to be contagious, the poor victim is brutally beaten to death with sticks, and the body bound to a small tree, far away from the village, generally

THE FIGURE OF A MURDERED MAN.

on some hill top, where the ghastly figure stands out in bold relief against the clear tropical sky.

Once, after a weary day's march, I became separated from my followers, and completely lost my way in the maze of native paths. It happened to be in a district where the people had for some time past been hostile to the officers of the Congo State. In order to obtain a more extensive view of the surrounding country, I climbed to the summit of an adjacent hill. Upon reaching the top, I was horrified to find, crowning the height before me, the figure of a murdered man bound to a rough branch that had been driven into the ground. His head had been crushed in by a heavy stone, and three hawks circled in the air around the ghastly scene. While gazing at this horrible sight, I could hear the sound of firing in the valley beneath. The

sun was sinking, and I should soon
darkness. I was unarmed, and my
ed with fears for my followers. I
what the sounds I heard might be a
their fate. But the scene and its
so strange fascination for me that
it without making a rough sketch
Steering my course for a fire
ing about two h ndred feet
cended the hillside in the dark-
glad to find that I had chanced
fire of my own followers.
go week consists of four
Nkonsu, Nkenge and Nsona.
which are usually
are named after
markets follow in
all the people of the
assemble in the
on the following
ble on an adja-
market place of
kets are usually
three miles apart
boring chiefs,
their laws are
mitted in the
is visited upon
anger. There is
which consist of

be surrounded by
mind was agitat-
knew not but
message to me of
surroundings had
I could not leave
in my note-book.
that I saw flicker-
beneath me, I des-
ness, and was
upon the camp
The Bakon-
days, Nkandu,
The market places,
situated on hill tops,
these days, and the
rotation. On Nkandu
neighboring villages
Nkandu market, and
day they again assem-
cent hill, which is the
Nkonsu. These mar-
situated about two or
and are presided over by the neigh-
who settle all disputes and see that
not infringed. No guns are per-
markets, and summary punishment
any one who draws a knife in
no recognized price for their wares,
all kinds of vegetable food in sea-

son, and principally manioc, bananas, sweet potatoes, yams, peanuts, peppers, egg-fruit and pine apples.   After the rainy season,
when the long grass is burnt, the rat season commences.   They
are caught in long, narrow basket-work traps, which are cylin-
drical in shape, and placed in such positions that when the grass
is set alight, the rats will run
into the traps, which are too
narrow for them to turn
around in.   They are then
killed, skewered and broiled,
as shown in my sketch.

Coarse salt is sold in a
thimble-like measure.   Fat
pork is sold in small portions
of about an ounce, the choice
fat being frequently fastened
on a long skewer, which, for
safe keeping, the butcher will
sometimes pin in his woolly
hair ; so that on a hot day the
valuable grease trickles over
his head and shoulders in a
way he considers extrava-
gant.

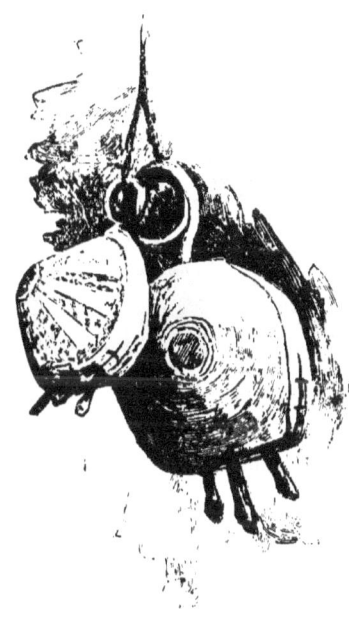

WOODEN PIG BELLS.

Under the shade of bushes, about a hundred yards from the
actual busy scene of the market, there are, perhaps, three or four
fat pigs wallowing in the dust and panting from the excessive
heat ; frequently, under an adjoining bush, may be seen poor,
dejected-looking slaves, tired and footsore, who have been brought
from some distance inland, either for sale in the markets or for

payment and tribute to the middlemen, who act for the natives in their ivory selling transactions with the Portuguese traders.

Under other bushes are lean and patient goats, tied to the branches, while their owners are away in the busy throng touting for customers; usually five goats are considered equivalent in value to one pig, and in some places, where pork is rare, a human slave is readily bartered for a fat hog.

A little further off, under the scanty shade of neighboring trees, are gathered little knots of convivial spirits, who sit with their legs doubled under them, round some knowing-looking old *nganga nkissi* (charm - doctor) who deftly serves *malafu*,

MALAFU GOURDS.

which is the sap of the palm tree, from a huge brown gourd held affectionately under his arm, pouring it into some old cracked and dirty mug, that, years ago, was taken by some native in part payment for the product he sold to the Portuguese traders on the coast. I remember once seeing a big, burly, evil-looking native, whose face bore every indication of rascality and brutishness, drinking *malafu* from such a mug, upon which was printed in gilded letters, " A Present to a Good Little Girl."

Under the influence of this *malafu*, which is rendered more potent by the fierce heat of the tropical sun, the *nganga* will grow garrulous, for the wily charm-doctor, in portioning out the palm wine, always retains a just appreciation of number one, and consequently he soon reaches a state of oblivious drunkenness, whilst the other boon-companions repeat scandal and say unkind things of their neighbors, and enter into maudlin discussions as to the relative price of locusts and white caterpillars, in the neighboring *Nsona* and *Nkandu* markets.

LUKUNGU STATION.

CHAPTER VII.

I FOUND myself stationed, in the year 1885, with one other white man, at Lukungu, which may be described as in the heart of the Bakongo country. Our attention was chiefly directed to inspiring the surrounding people with confidence in our friendly intentions, and in endeavoring to induce them to act as carriers in the service of the Free State.

To effect these objects, it often became necessary for one of us to go out for several days at a time among the neighboring villages, while the other would stay at home to guard the station and look after the men.

This duty more often fell to me than to my companion, and in my journeyings among them, stopping a night in one village and then passing on to the next, I had many opportunities of studying the native character, and of becoming very friendly with the different chiefs of the neighborhood.

Some fifteen miles from Lukungu rises the highest mountain of the Bakongo country, a hill known as Mongwa Bidi, which towers probably three thousand feet above the valley, its bare, rocky crown being a prominent landmark for fully fifty miles around. I determined on climbing this hill, and set off one morning from my camp at its base to scale its rugged sides. After some hours of a most toilsome ascent, I succeeded in gaining the summit, and, instead of finding a precipitous descent on the other side, similar to that I had ascended, I saw, stretching for miles before me, a richly wooded table-land dotted with villages nestling in groves of palm-trees, and surrounded by bright green patches of cultivated land. Continuing my journey, I speedily arrived at the nearest of them, and was soon surrounded by a crowd of people of a somewhat different type I had been accustomed to meet in the lowlands. Wearied with my long day's tramp and the fatigue of climbing, I requested permission to sleep in their village, and that they would furnish me with food until I should be able to rejoin my own men, who would be anxiously awaiting me at the far-off foot of Mongwa Bidi.

In a few minutes, I observed a crowd coming along the main street of the village toward me, headed by the chief, who was arrayed in a loin-cloth of blue and white check cotton, while the majority of his subjects wore the coarse yellow *mbadi* cloth made of fiber of the pine-apple stalk or of the palm-tree.

Seating himself on the grass mat which was spread on the

MONGWA BIDI

ground in front of the hut to which I had been conducted on making known my desire to sleep in the village, the chief requested me to imitate his example; and then the crowd of followers formed themselves into a semicircle behind him, squatting upon their haunches.

An urchin of twelve or so then leaned forward and placed a black earthenware pot, covered with green leaves which served as a lid, on the mat in front of me ; and the chief, a dignified looking fellow, with an upper lip dyed pale brown from frequent snuff-taking, commanded his chief adviser to inform me, in a set speech, that he was very pleased to see a white man in his country ; that he had sometimes heard of me from people who had been to Lukungu, and much more to the same effect ; and, in conclusion, to say that he had much pleasure in begging my acceptance of the accompanying pot of food ; and, taking off the leaves, he revealed to my astonished and horrified gaze a mass of white and green caterpillars already roasted by having been held over a fire in green cup-shaped leaves. This dainty and delicate repast was one the chief—whose name I learned was Ngudi Nkama, literally "Parent of a Hundred"—highly esteemed, and he fancied I should be delighted to partake of the succulent and juicy dish ere going to sleep.

I slept that night on the bamboo frame, raised a few inches above the ground, which serves as a bed in all Bakongo houses ; or rather I endeavored to sleep while the mosquitoes took their Sunday dinner off the strange white man who had come up among them. I was hungry, too, for the eggs, which had been procured after my refusal to eat the caterpillars, were neither large nor plentiful ; and those raw eggs, assisted by a piece of *kwanga*, formed but a poor meal after a hard day's walking and climbing.

The natives were drumming on a goat-skin stretched tightly across the mouth of a hollowed-out log, and dancing round a fire lighted in their midst, one man singing a refrain, while others took up the chorus; and the mingled sound of the voices and the distant beating of other drums in neighboring villages helped to keep me awake. This noise had continued four hours or so, and

I judged it was be-tween ten and eleven o'clock, when a great outcry at the further end of the village caused the drumming and singing to cease suddenly, and brought me out from my hut into the moonlit square in front, which was fast emptying of peo-

MUSICAL INSTRUMENTS OF THE BAKONGO "BICHI."

ple, who appeared to be all hurrying down in the direction of the disturbance. I followed them, and was soon in the midst of an excited throng, listening to the recital of what had happened. It appeared that one of the women, requiring water, had taken her earthenware pot and descended the steep hill to the spring some two or three hundred yards off. She had taken a young girl with her as company on this journey, and as they approached the water, a leopard had sprung from a clump of bushes on the far side of the stream and knocked the poor little creature down. The woman fled, shrieking, up the hill, and fortunately unpursued by the leopard, when her cries of terror soon attracted the crowd I beheld around me. The men were many of them already armed with flint lock muskets and bows and arrows, and running back for my rifle, which lay beside my bed, I hurried after them down the hill. Fearing the leopard might escape if we all came down by the same path, I told some of the men to go off by the left and get to the other side of the spring, while I came down the track the women had pursued.

On reaching the water, we found the body of the girl terribly torn where the paw of the brute had struck her between the shoulders, and her breast lacerated also, as though the animal had, after knocking her down, turned the body over.

There were no signs of the leopard, and after searching about in all the thickets near the spring, we returned to the village, bearing the girl's body with us. On examining her at the firelight above, we discovered that the claws had penetrated deep into her flesh, and we had very little hope of her recovering. She was carried off to one of the huts, and the *nganga* came to endeavor to bind up the wounds and stop the bleeding, but ere morning the girl was dead. She never regained consciousness. We wondered why the leopard had not injured her more. He must have been startled immediately after striking her, although only a very ferocious beast would have attempted to attack two persons together.

In the morning, saddened by the event of the night, I left the village to return to my own men down at the foot of Mongwa Bidi. My path led me past the scene of the previous night's tragedy, and as I passed the stream and commenced climbing the slight ascent which led up to the level of the table-land beyond, I heard a noise in the bushes to my left. Looking there, I saw the figure of a man pushing his way with difficulty through the trees and thick undergrowth. On emerging, he came toward me, and

E

I then saw that he was bleeding from several cuts across the chest and shoulders. I soon learned the cause of these wounds. The native had been returning from a neighboring village the night before, just at the moment the leopard sprang upon the girl ; and, as the woman fled up the hill, he appeared upon the scene. The leopard, hearing him, turned, and seeing the advancing figure of the man, it ·sprang upon him just at the moment he raised his musket and fired. The shot took effect, and the leopard, badly wounded, made off, while the native—a courageous fellow and a famous hunter, as I afterward discovered—seeing that it would escape him, and not wishing to lose such noble game, made after it without thinking of the girl. Some half mile away, he came upon the brute, and having had time to reload his gun, he again fired at close quarters. This time the leopard sprang and grappled him, and for a moment he had thought all was lost ; but gathering himself together, he dealt the wounded brute a fearful blow on the skull with the butt end of his gun, and forced it to loose its hold, when, again swinging his gun, he crushed in its skull completely.

He fell, exhausted and bleeding from numerous wounds, beside the beast, and lay there, almost unconscious, until morning, when the warmth and light of the sun revived him sufficiently to enable him to crawl off to a neighboring brook, and after refreshing himself there, and bathing his wounds, he had managed to stagger along to the place where I saw him.

I helped him back up to the village, where, on his story being told, a party immediately set off in search of the dead body of the leopard, which was carried in upon a pole by two men.

The native who had done this brave deed was regarded as a very fine fellow by his companions, and the claws and teeth of the leopard he strung together and wore round his neck as a collar, to tell all men of his achievement.

I subsequently saw him several times at Lukungu Station, whither he came, with others of the same village, to get cloth for the men who were to act as carriers for Bula Matadi (Stanley), and we were very good friends, for I always had an admiration for the courage of this fellow in tackling a wounded leopard single-handed.

This story relates an instance of pluck rarely to be met with among the tribes of the Lower Congo ; for although they are great hunters of antelope and smaller game, they draw the line at elephants, buffaloes and leopards, endeavoring to trap those beasts into pitfalls, where they can kill them at leisure and in safety.

CHAPTER VIII.

AVERAGE DAY'S MARCH—MAYALA MBEMBA (EAGLE'S WINGS) MY NATIVE NAME—A CASUAL OBSERVER'S FIRST IMPRESSIONS—I SHOOT AN OLD BULL ELEPHANT—A BANQUET.

THE average day's march of a white man on the road from Matadi to Stanley Pool, is from ten to fifteen miles. Some walk even a shorter distance than this. The natives have been known to travel as many as thirty miles in a day, with a load of sixty-five or seventy pounds on their shoulders, over a very rocky and hilly part of the road ; but such marches are quite exceptional, and fifteen to twenty miles are the outside limit of what they care to attempt when carrying loads.

They have a great admiration for any exhibition of personal strength, skill or endurance, and the white man who can shoot an elephant or buffalo, or walk some tremendously long distance, is sure of winning their regard.

I earned my name of *Mayala Mbemba, i. e.,* "The Wings of the Eagle," from having once accomplished the journey from Kimpete to Lukungu in one day—a distance of forty miles, over a wearisome and fatiguing road.

After a very long and weary tramp I got into Lukungu in the night—after every one had gone to bed—and not wishing to waken my companion, I lay down for the night on our small dining-table, where the boys, who came in the early morning to prepare breakfast, found me snoring comfortably, to their vast astonishment. My carriers had learned on arriving at the Kwilu

of my not having tarried there, and to their dismay could
find no traces of me at the spot I had named as our camping-place
for that day. Two days later they reached Lukungu, where they
learned of my arrival on the same day that I had quitted Kimpete,
and they said I must
have had the wings of
an eagle to perform the
journey in that time.
The name stuck to me,
and during the remain-
der of my stay among
the Bakongo, I became
quite popular on ac-
count of my by no
means extraordinary
performance. Proba-
bly the fact that it was
a white man who had
beaten them at their
own particular avoca-
tion, astonished them
most, for the carriers
pride themselves on
their walking powers.
The idea had gained
ground among the na-

A BAKONGO HUT.

tives that the *mindeli*, the white men, were incapable of much
exertion, as they had been accustomed too often to see poor fellows
suffering from the effects of the climate, painfully toiling along,
with livid faces and bodies bent from fatigue, over the long hills

and through the deep valleys of thick, saturated grass ; or them selves had borne upon their own sturdy shoulders and heads in a roughly made hammock, some pitiful wreck of a gallant youth, who left home six months before, full of health and vigor, only to find himself now being hurried down to the coast in the faint hope that he might live to reach the deck of the homeward-bound steamer.

To the casual observer, the tribes who inhabit the cataract region appear careless, indolent beings. He sees them gathered in groups in the market-place or in the doorways of their huts, basking in the sun the livelong day, and it is with the greatest difficulty that he can rouse them to the slightest exertion when he needs their aid in the work of an expedition. Yet beneath the apathetic exterior is hidden a certain native shrewdness, the unexpected display of which has, on several occasions, surprised and amused me.

A certain perverse logic furnishes them with inexhaustible reasons and excuses when they find themselves in a difficulty ; for instance, the weary hunter who has tramped over hill and dale in search of an elephant which existed only in the imagination of the native tracker, will be lured on mile after mile by the assertion of the wily impostor at each stage of his fruitless quest, that, having gone so far, he may as well continue, for it is surely better to march on a short distance further where he knows he may find an elephant. than to return to camp where he knows he certainly will not.

One morning, in the early dawn before sunrise, I was awakened by the gruff voice of a native, who, thrusting his head through the flap of my tent, said :

"*O Mayala Mbemba nswalu nswalu Zinzau zikale zinavave !*"

(Quick ! quick ! Eagle's Wings ; there are elephants here !) I was
on my feet in a moment, and hastily catching up my rifle and
ammunition belt, I followed my guide through the dim morning
mist for some distance. Soon we met two native women, who
were standing on a high rock, gazing intently upon a dense patch
of forest at the junction of two hills. In whispers we arranged
our plans. The two women were to proceed to the further edge of
the forest, and the man was to take up a position near the rock,
whilst I went down to the swamp in the valley to meet the
elephants, as they would in all probability take that direction
when aroused by the shouts and yells of the three natives, whom
I had carefully instructed to give me sufficient time to take up my
position in the swamp before commencing the alarm. I had just
reached the swamp, when I heard the distant shouts and cries of
the natives, followed soon afterward by the crashing of branches
in the forest, which indicated that the elephants were startled. A
few minutes elapsed, when suddenly there emerged the huge form
of an old bull elephant, whose skin hung in wrinkled folds. He
stood opposite me at the verge of the forest, shaking his head and
flapping his great ragged ears, and appeared dazed by the sudden
burst of light after the darkness of the forest.

The yells of the natives continued, and the startled elephant
chafed and became irritated.

Apparently he objected to leaving the quietude of the forest to
travel in the open. But the cries on the hill-top warned
him of danger. Raising my rifle, I aimed for the brain, and fired.

When the smoke cleared off, he was on the ground. As I ran
forward a few paces, thinking my shot had proved fatal, the
monster recovered himself, and in a moment was on his legs
again. Curling up his trunk, and arching his back, he squealed

with rage. My bullet had missed its mark, and had, apparently, only grazed the temple.

The enraged brute retreated a few paces, and catching sight of a small tree, about six inches in diameter, he coiled his trunk around the stem and hoisted it up by the roots, throwing it high in the air, and completely enveloping himself in a cloud of dust. I fired a second time, and was more fortunate in my aim, for the brute staggered an instant and fell heavily forward, shot through the brain.

The natives who resided in the neighboring villages, upon hearing gun-shots, were soon attracted to the spot. Straggling parties were to be seen in all directions, wending their way in single file toward the carcass, the men armed with long knives to cut up the meat, and the women bearing *matets*—long baskets made from palm fronds—in which to carry the meat home.

I stood aside, watching the excited throng of natives gather around the dead elephant, their eyes distended with delight at the sight of so much meat. I myself was disappointed, for I found the elephant was a solitary "rogue," without tusks. A tall old chief, attired in a red cotton loin-cloth and a smoking-cap, resting his arms on his long-barreled, flint-lock gun, watched me keenly for some time. At last he said, in his soft, rich language :

"Why is the white man so sad looking ? Is he not satisfied that he alone has killed such a big elephant? See its size ; it is truly a monster."

I replied :

"Yes ; but see, he has no tusks. I have had all this trouble for nothing. What gain is it for me to shoot an elephant without ivory ?"

"Ah, yes, you speak true words ; you have not obtained any

"I AIMED FOR THE BRAIN, AND FIRED." (Page 75.)

valuable ivory. But why should you be sad? See the meat there is for us!"

The scene that followed was wild and disgusting, as the men hacked and gashed the still warm, steaming flesh, heaving it in reeking lumps to their women, who were eagerly crowding around, quarreling and fighting with one another like hungry dogs. Now and then a bigger lump of meat than usual would be thrown among them, and they would all rush forward and literally tear it to pieces in their wild greed.

Soon they were all besmeared with blood; and the men, naked and perspiring, had hacked their way into the very vitals of the carcass, where their sickening operations were only interrupted by occasional scrimmages, as some too enterprising butcher would receive a gash from the keen-edged knife of his more phlegmatic neighbor in remonstrance.

At sunset I revisited the scene; there was not a native left; the grass was bloody and trodden down all around the bare skeleton, upon which there was scarcely an atom of meat left. A few carrion birds hovered overhead. The bones were scraped clean and white, and the great arched ribs and massive bones of the monster that had been so powerful but a few hours before reminded me then of the orthodox elephant skeleton of our natural history museums.

CHAPTER IX.

SYSTEM OF MANUAL TRANSPORT—DIFFICULTIES IN ROUTE—THEFT—PAYMENT IN CLOTH,
BEADS AND BRASS WIRE—ARDENT SPIRITS PREFERRED—DOUBTFUL ADVANTAGES—
LOCAL HOSTILITIES—BELLES OF BWENDE.

THE present system of supplying up-river stations with
merchandise, provisions, and all the thousand and one little
items essential to carrying on the work of civilization and
commerce among the barbarous peoples of the interior, is tedious,
unreliable and expensive in the extreme. Every bale of cloth or
case of hardware or box of provisions, destined for the stations on
the Upper Congo, must be carried a distance of two hundred and
ten to two hundred and twenty miles on the heads and shoulders
of natives engaged for this service among the Bakongo tribes
of the cataract region ; and the competition between the various
commercial houses and missions having posts to be supplied and
steamers to be kept running on the Upper Congo, as well as the
necessities of the government, which always has a great store of
goods at Matadi, the point of debarkation from Europe on the
lower river, situated below the first of the cataracts, awaiting
transport to Leopoldville on Stanley Pool, where the river again
becomes navigable, renders the work of getting a sufficient
number of carriers one of much difficulty.

The people available for this arduous labor are confined,
generally speaking, to the districts of Lukungu and Manyanga,
situated midway between Matadi and Stanley Pool, on the south
bank of the Congo ; although a considerable number of porters

have recently been ob-
tained from the northern
bank opposite Manyanga,
as also from the districts
of Ngombe, Lutete and
Nzungi, nearer Stanley

Pool. These latter dis-
tricts, however, are, as a
rule, pretty well occupied
with their own trade con-
cerns, the majority of the
young men and slaves
being employed by their
chiefs in the transport of
ivory, purchased by them
from the Bateke, on the
shores of Stanley Pool, to
the European trading
houses on the lower river,
and they have not, there-
fore, many days to devote
to the work of carrying
up the white man's loads.
    From the date of
leaving Matadi until it

A BAKONGO CARRIER.

safely reaches Leopoldville, a load of merchandise will undergo
fully a month's, sometimes four or five months' delay on the road,
suffering from frequent immersion in the numerous rivers to be
crossed, or from repeated wettings during the rainfalls, which in
these regions more resemble waterspouts than ordinary outpour-
ings of the clouds.   During the greater part of this time the load
will be jolted and jogged about on the head of the native carrier,
as he wearily climbs high, stony hills only to descend again into

BAKONGO CARRIERS EN ROUTE.

deep ravines, or to traverse, by a narrow footpath, hot and steamy
from overhanging grass, a small plain intersected by rapid torrents
tearing their way through the red clay soil, amid a maze of rich
vegetation, which shelters their cool waters from the burning rays
of the sun, to fall at last into the great gorge through which the
Congo roars and foams upon its troubled journey to the Atlantic
—the deep booming of its cataracts often breaking upon the

ear as the caravan route approaches places within a mile or two of its banks.

Day after day the carrier trudges along, his sixty-five or seventy-pound bale often getting a rude shock as he drops it on the ground, while he rests himself stretched out in the grateful shade of some grove of trees, or partakes of a scanty "snack" of *kwanga* (cassava pudding) or a roast plantain, flavored with a handful of scorched ground-nuts, all washed down by a

S. MANYANGA.

draught from the neighboring brook, ere again setting out on his journey. Should the load he carries contain bottles of wine or brandy, as is often the case when medical comforts for the poor fellows buried in the swampy forests of the interior are being sent up river, there is every chance of its entire contents being smashed to fragments long before it reaches the midway stations of Manyanga or Lukungu; but in the event of carelessness being noticeable in the manner of carrying the load, or marks of unnecessary violence showing on its exterior, the receiving agent at either of those stations will open the case and reveal its damaged contents to the carrier, and deduct from his pay an amount equivalent to the loss. This method of punishment has caused the natives to be extremely careful in the way they handle any loads whose contents they have been warned at Matadi are liable to be broken if not treated with care; for it proves indeed an unsatisfactory termination to a long and weary tramp of over two hundred miles—down from Manyanga, empty handed, to get a load, and then up from Matadi, with bale or box, as the case may be—to find that all the expected pay for this work must go to satisfy the hard-hearted and relentless white man, who contend that a case of twelve bottles of brandy smashed and empty is but poorly compensated for in Central Africa by the retention of four pieces of cheap cotton or colored handkerchiefs from the person who caused the loss.

The payment to the carriers is made in kind—in cheap cottons, blue glass beads, brass wire, or any of the various trifles that please the savage mind—although the prevailing standard of value is a piece of hankerchiefs, consisting of a strip numbering twelve handkerchiefs, each strip being known as a *kimbundi* or "whole cloth" by the natives. Four such pieces represent the payment for the carriage of a load of sixty-five pounds up as far as Manyanga, and three more are required to requite the services of the man taking it on to Stanley Pool; the total price of these pieces and of the other cloth previously given as rations to each carrier, brings up the cost of transport per load from Matadi to Stanley Pool to one pound sterling ; representing from thirty-five to forty pounds per ton of merchandise.

But with the people who live near the white trader's " factories," along the sea-coast, the fiery, ardent spirits, prepared expressly for the African trade, are more popular than any other form of payment.

"We prefer being paid in bottles of gin or rum, for we can sell a drink, take a drink ourselves, and afterward, when all is finished, barter the empty bottles."

"It appears to me," said I, to a native carrier who had expressed himself in this way, "that you are able to dispose of everything to advantage in such payments except the headache which attends your 'Take a drink.'"

He paused and reflected for a moment, and then as the idea struck him for the first time, a smile lit up his simple face, and he replied :

"*Kedika kwandi, Ekh! Ekh! mundili nduku bene.* (That's true, oh the white man's cleverness!)"

In addition to all the labor and cost of getting carriers, and to the delay often experienced in the receipt of loads, owing to the carriers having "sat down" for a month or two in their villages *en route*, or gambled their rations in

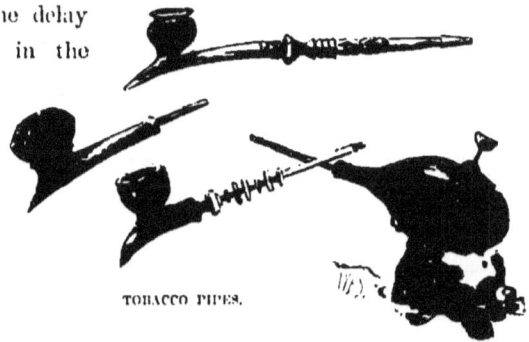

TOBACCO PIPES.

some games resembling chuck-farthing during a halt, and being unable or unwilling to continue their journey without further "rations," there is occasionally great risk of the loss of an entire

caravan of goods by theft among the porters themselves, or from
an attack by some petty chief along the road who is at feud with
the government of the Free State, and takes this as an opportunity of being avenged on the white man.

Such outbreaks fortunately are growing fewer and fewer along
the route of the caravans, as we style a body of carriers under
their head man or *kapita*; but a few years since there was always
a "palaver" with the natives somewhere or other along the line

MODE OF INHALING TOBACCO SMOKE.

of march.   Either a native market had been invaded by a gang of
Zanzibari or Houssa soldiers on the march from station to station,
unaccompanied by a white officer, and an outbreak had resulted in

the road past that particular spot being closed, until punishment inflicted on the obstructive village brought its chief to his senses,
and caused the road to be re-opened ; or a conflict between two
neighboring villages threw the entire neighborhood into a state of
the most tremendous excitement, and while the furious battle
raged by an interchange of "champion long distance" shots from
two opposite hillsides across an intervening valley, no carrier
would attempt to pass the scene of the fight.

VIEW DOWN THE CONGO AT MANYANGA.

Day after day and week after week would this state of affairs
continue, little execution being done on either side, until mutual
exhaustion of ammunition caused a cessation of hostilities, only to
be renewed probably when the return of a couple of caravans hastily dispatched down to the lower river with produce to change at
the factories for more gunpowder and flintlock guns, enabled both
sides to re-enter the field with refreshed vigor, and by the time
they had settled their little dispute and slaughtered the pig of

peace—pork, cold, roast or boiled, playing a prominent part in the settlement of all affairs of importance, domestic or public, among the Bakongo—all semblance of a transport system on *that* part of

A BAKONGO GIRL.

the road had entirely disappeared, and it required persuasion and diplomacy on the part of the State officials of Lukungu, to set their carriers' fears at rest, and start fresh caravans on the road to Matadi.

BWENDE BELLES.

On one occasion, some two years ago, a large caravan of men from the north bank of the Congo had taken loads at Manyanga for Stanley Pool, consisting mainly of material for one of the steamers then being put together at Leopoldville, among which was a quantity of copper boiler-tubing and iron piping.

Having got well out of the ken of the State officials of Manyanga, this gang of innocents called a halt, and after having duly weighed the *pros* and *cons* of the undertaking they meditated, asserted the inordinate over-weight of the loads they had been forced to take at Manyanga, and the length of the road to the Pool, and finally confessed that copper was a very valuable and enticing metal, and looked peculiarly lustrous in conjunction with a black complexion, they incontinently bolted with all their loads to their distant villages in the Bwende hills, on the north bank. Some short time afterward, search was made by the state officers for the missing copper tubes, which were then badly wanted for the completion of the steamer's boiler ; but no sign of them could be discovered along the caravan route, and it was only as gradual native reports filtered into Manyanga of the marvelous display of copper necklets and leg rings and iron bracelets by the dusky beauties of Bwende on market days, that the horrible truth at length dawned upon the official mind at Manyanga, and steps were taken to recover what might yet be saved from the melting process to which a great part of the steamer's fittings had been subjected in the task of converting it into jewelry for the fair sex of Bwende.

CHAPTER X.

A BLAND ACKNOWLEDGMENT OF THEFT—THE CONGO RAILWAY—SURVEY—ADVENTURES
OF SURVEYING PARTY—ELEPHANTS AND HOSTILE NATIVES—THE DOCTOR'S DILEMMA
—PROSPECT OF SUCCESS FOR THE RAILWAY.

THE punishment meted out by the State Station of Manyanga to the various villages around it, for thefts
committed upon caravans of goods passing through their
precincts, was often summary enough in the early days of the
effort to found a transport system. One village, that of Mafiela,
had particularly distinguished itself by its persistent and often
successful attempts to pillage the State caravans. It was three
times burned to the ground by the officer in charge of Manyanga,
and three times successively rebuilt, a work of no great labor, by
the natives, on the conclusion of hostilities. In one of the
intervals between these reconstruction schemes, I happened to be
passing the site of the ruined village, and gazing round on the
scene of destruction presented by the charred huts, uprooted
plantain and banana-trees, and the withered, burnt-up foliage of
the palms and other environing trees, I inquired from a native
who was standing near, the cause of this desolation.

" Oh," replied he, " the white men of Bula Matada (the name
of Stanley, now synonymous with that of the Free State fort he
founded, which the natives regard as being his entire creation, and
the white officials as his slaves or children) came up from down
there "—pointing to Manyanga, some two or three miles below by
the edge of the Congo—" and burned us out, because they said we
had robbed one of their caravans."

" And did you steal from it ? " I inquired.

A smile of intense satisfaction rippled and broadened over the countenance of the native as he burst out in reply :

" *Minge, minge,*" (plenty, plenty) spreading out his arms, with curving fingers, to denote the extent of the depredations he and his friends had inflicted on the white man's bales of cloth. Even the woe and affliction of the present could not seem to efface the glory and joy of that happy past from his face or mind, and, like the figure in Wordsworth's great ode which came " trailing clouds of fiery splendor " behind it, he reveled in the recollections of that vision of his own noble form trailing clouds of many-colored cotton splendors behind it, as he returned from that successful raid upon the goods of Bula Matadi.

As a rule, however, despite instances to the contrary, such as the preceding, the Bakongo natives are wonderfully honest in the manner of their transport of the loads intrusted to their charge ; and it is rarely that any bale or box is tampered with *en route*, or that the loads are not all brought in safety to their destination.

Such is a brief outline of the system, by means of which the Upper Congo is at present supplied with the essentials to the existence of the stations established along its course. A railway to overcome the difficulties of this mode of transport, to run through the cataract region, and connect Matadi with the Pool, has been mooted ever since Stanley gave to the world his story of the " Founding of the Free State," but it was not until two years ago the project took tangible form, when a surveying expedition, consisting of two parties of Belgian civil engineers, under a director who was an old officer of the Belgian army, commenced operations through the stretch of country that extends to the south of the caravan route along the banks of the Congo, so as to find a less deeply indented line of route than that near the river, over the plains and gently rising uplands, which were believed to lie in that direction.

For two years the work of survey was carried on under great difficulties through an unknown country, for immediately to the right or left of the ordinary carrier-trail the map of the Lower Congo was a blank, and the engineers found themselves working in the dark, not knowing in what description of country, whether hilly, or filled with hostile natives, the next week's survey might bring them.

But little progress was made during the first year, the gigantic hills and the rugged nature of the ground around Matadi proving no easy barrier to surmount in the work of mapping out a road practicable for a railway.

With the commencement of the second campaign, in the summer of '88, the work advanced more rapidly. The following descriptions I gathered from a friend who was attached to the surveying column:

A point had been reached that brought the expedition face to face with an immense precipice of rock towering one thousand feet above the plain, and extending north and south as far as the eye could see. It was necessary to divert the line of survey much to the south, to avoid this obstacle to further progress. And this flank movement brought the expedition into a country where white men had not before penetrated, and over whose grassy plains, broken by little lakes and clumps of thick bush, wandered numerous herds of elephants. To enable the engineers to obtain an un-interrupted view of the land around them, and so gauge the inequalities of its surface by means of their instruments and measuring poles held up at various points within view, it became

necessary to burn the long grass which covers the face of the country in all directions—a task the natives reserve for the month of August, when it has attained the necessary dryness, at the termination of the *nsiru* or dry season.

The natives resented this forestalling of their plans, and many remonstrances were carried from the neighboring villages to the engineers ; for the natives attach much importance to this grass-burning, as it supplies them with a plentiful harvest of rats, which are driven into traps by the flames. But still, day after day, the white men went on with the work, and long lines of smoke drifting across the horizon, through which swept hawks and eagles innumerable, darting occasionally almost into the flaming mass below to strike a rat or snake endeavoring to escape the flames, marked the extent of that day's survey. Remonstrances were followed by threats, and the natives more than once assembled to do battle for their hunting rights, but timely presents of cloth, or the rapid removal of the surveying camps to points further on, prevented a conflict.

The elephants liked the fires no better than the natives, and often during the work the labors of the party would be interrupted by the appearance of a herd of these huge brutes marching out of some clump of trees within a few hundred yards of the surveying party, and making off across the plains, pursued by the shots of the excited engineers, who had hastily thrown their instruments aside to grasp their rifles.

At one camping-place the tents were pitched in the center of a great plain near the only pools of water to be found for a considerable distance. At night, about seven o'clock while dinner was being eaten, the black servants and carriers of the expedition came rushing in among the tents and cooking pots from their camp-fire, crying out that the elephants were upon them. Every white man seized his rifle, and, running out to the fires of the men, some forty or fifty yards off, they perceived in the darkness several huge creatures making for the water.

A fusilade was at once opened upon them from five or six rifles, but in the dim light it was impossible to aim correctly; however, one elephant was shot dead within a few yards of the tents, and several of the others wounded, as their trumpeting in their flight plainly indicated. Not satisfied with this reception, the next morning they reappeared in force, and again came down toward the tents, and it was only after repeated shots had been fired at them that they made off. This second herd numbered twenty-three, the leader being a huge old bull, who pioneered the way across the plain.

That night they returned to the charge, determined to dare everything for a drink ; or, perhaps the new-comers were strangers to the morning's disturbance, and were only coming to an accustomed pool. They, too, were routed, but without leaving any of their number behind as trophies of the engineers' good aim. For several days the expedition continued in the land of elephants, herds of the creatures often coming up close to the surveying party, ere they found out their mistake and took to flight. One day, the doctor of the expedition, being out on a botanizing excursion, had occasion to enter a small wood in search of specimens. Laying his shot gun, the only weapon he carried with him, by his side, he sat down to enjoy a few minutes' smoking, when from the belt of timber in front of him he saw emerge the leader of a herd of elephants. Counting them as they issued from the trees, he discovered that the herd numbered fifty-five—an enormous assemblage of elephants, truly--and for fully a quarter of an hour

he continued to watch them unobserved, until they had dispersed and scattered through the forest. The doctor was seated on a hill-top fronting the portion of the wood where the elephants were, and quite screened from their gaze; and, situated as he was, they could not get his scent. At last, one old fellow came toward him—the others had by this time all disappeared—and as the solitary brute approached him, the doctor gave way to the excitement of the moment, and raising his shot gun, he fired straight at the elephant's forehead. The charge of duck-shot hit the fleshy part of the trunk, and, trumpeting shrilly in surprise and fear, and spluttering blood all over the trees and grass within a few paces of the doctor, the elephant made off after the rest of the herd, while the doctor was not slow in putting as long a distance as possible between himself and his late antagonist. He returned to camp breathless, to be received with incredulous smiles from every one to whom he related his adventure.

On arriving at the Nkissi river, which is the largest of the southern tributaries of the Congo from the sea up to the mouth of the Kassai, the expedition quitted the game country, and entered a broken land of ravines and forest, extending for fifty miles or so to near Stanley Pool.

At every village and market-place the advent of the white men was hailed by crowds of natives, although, as a rule, few women could be seen in their midst. A lurking suspicion that there might be trouble with these strange people, who went through the country doing what no man comprehended, with curious red and white painted poles—the surveying measures—kept the villagers from being too friendly; and often the early advances of friendship were changed into sullen distrust or openly expressed hostility, as rumors adverse to the characters and intentions of the white men were circulated by the *ngangas*, who are ever among the first to oppose the coming of the white men, fearing that their iniquitous influence may be weakened by the new ideas and inducements to work that follow in their train.

Descending the valley of the Lukaya, the expedition emerged upon the level plain that extends from the shores of Stanley Pool to the foot of the chain of hills which surrounds that expansion of the Congo. The preliminary survey had thus been successfully ended, and at the time I write, the first steps in the actual construction of the line are being undertaken at Matadi, and it is hoped that in a space of five years, and at a cost of little over one million pounds sterling, the work will be completed, and the secrets of tropical Africa, with the vast natural wealth of the Congo basin, laid bare to the gaze of the civilized world.

A BAKONGO'S GRAVE.

PART II.
UPPER CONGO.

CHAPTER I.

BOLOBO—A FERTILE COUNTRY—SACRIFICE OF HUMAN LIFE—MORE CRUEL THAN CANNIBALS
—COVENANT SEALED BY THE MURDER OF A SLAVE—CHARM-DOCTOR—A CHIEF
QUENCHES HIS THIRST—BULLETS EXTRACTED—THE BANKUNDU PEOPLE—EUELU—THE
NOMAD BAKUMBE.

SITUATED about six hundred miles in the interior from the
mouth of the Congo, is a fine, fertile country, well wooded
and watered, where every kind of game to be found in this
latitude of Western Africa abounds. Elephants, buffaloes, hippopotami, antelopes, wild pigs and guinea-fowl, red-legged partridge
and quail among the birds, are to be met with in abundance on
the grassy plains or among the forested hills of this district,
which is known as Bolobo, and is populated by a large and influential tribe of keen traders. These people, although not actually
cannibals, are, beyond doubt, one of the most cruel races met
with in this part of Central Africa.

They seem to take the keenest delight in the sacrifice of
human life, and the execution of their slaves is considered an
advertisement of their wealth. As this is a thickly peopled country, some dark deed of barbarism is taking place almost every
day, in connection with their inhuman ceremonies. Sometimes
slaves are decapitated upon the death of a chief, so that their
spirits may accompany that of the deceased potentate into the
other world, to add prestige in the form of a spiritual retinue.
At other times, a slave is brutally slaughtered by an enraged
master, for some slight act of disobedience. In that case, the

offender is pounced upon, hurled to the ground, and his head hacked from his body.

One of their most cruel ceremonies is that in connection with the settlement of long standing disagreements. It frequently happens that two sections of a tribe, for some family reason, entertain a bitter grudge against each other. This bitterness lasts until perhaps one or more of the influential members die, when the rest of the community, weary of the feud, decide amongst themselves to come to a settlement. A council of inquiry is accordingly held, and the most influential chiefs of the surrounding country are invited to attend, and the representatives of the two parties at variance have then the opportunity of stating their case, and receiving a verdict at the hands of the assembled chiefs, who decide which party is guilty and inflict a fine according to the nature of the case. And when this has been satisfactorily concluded, some incident is required by both parties to remind them of the covenant. Very often, on these occasions, a slave is purchased; the bones of his arms and legs are broken; he is carried to some open, well-known spot, generally a cross-road; a hole is dug, and he is placed in it, the earth being filled in and well trodden down around him, so as to leave his head just above the surface. Any person found giving him either food or water is liable to be served in the same way, and so he is left to die a lingering, painful death.

The greatest enemy to the slave's happiness is the Nganga Nkissi, or "charm-doctor." It is the same here as with the Bakongo tribes of the cataract region of the Lower Congo. Upon the death of any one of importance, it is always supposed that some evil influence has been at work, and it is to the "charm-doctor" that the duty is delegated of finding out the offender.

A VILLAGE SCENE AT BOLOBO

As a rule, some poor slave is selected, and more often than not, suffers death in consequence.

It is not difficult to distinguish the Nganga Nkissi. He wears a variety of heavy anklets and bangles, which are composed of brass, iron, or copper, and always has many bells hung around his waist, in addition to which he is decorated with little packets of befeathered charms hanging under his arms. He is invariably adorned with different-colored paint stripes about his body and arms, and assumes a deep and husky tone of voice.

Unless engaged in professional duties, the charm doctor rarely speaks to any one. The welfare of a whole village, is, to a certain extent, in this man's hands. As he is supposed to be possessed of supernatural power, his aid is constantly being sought. When two villages are about to make war, all the charm-doctors are particularly busy in making charms, and finding out by means of mysterious communings with the spirit world what is likely to be the result of the fight. Some warriors are anxious to have a charm that will protect them from a spear thrust; others from a gun shot; and some drink a magical compound that will save them from an arrow wound. They visit the Nganga, state their wants, and, after paying his demands, receive in return some small charm with full instructions as to their future course of life. These charms consist, as a rule, of small pieces of stone, beads, shells, dried flies, nuts and beans, in fact, any rubbish that the fetich-man can scrape together. Some of each of these articles are tied up in a small piece of cloth, into which three or four feathers are placed, to give them something of a mystic appearance; it is then attached to a string and hung around the warrior's shoulders; but this, however, is not in itself sufficient; there are restrictions and slight devotional duties to be attended to. For instance, the fetich-man will instruct a client, before eating in the morning, to put a mark of red chalk on his face ; and before drinking, to tie a piece of string around his big toe, stick a bean in between his second and third toes ; hold a knife in his hand, and

A CHIEFTAIN OF BOLOBO.

have somebody close by with his eyes shut, and another to poke at him with the branch of a tree.

Some chiefs, who take particular care of themselves, knowing the uncertainty of their popularity, and how liable they are to be put out of the way, are good customers to these charm-doctors and have the most extensive devotions to attend to. A big chief at Busindi has to go through the following ceremonies every time he seeks to quench his thirst. He himself is compelled to hold a leaf in his mouth, and put three stones in the cup from which he is about to drink. He has to shut his eyes whilst drinking, and not take his cup from his lips until he has drained it. One man has to hold the jar containing the palm wine, another the drinking-cup, and a third passes it to him when filled, and " bumpers " only are offered to a chief of Busindi. Two men rattle rough native bells throughout the ceremony, and one woman is deputed to stand behind and clasp the chief about the waist. Others, kneeling down before him, shut their eyes and clap their hands. Thus the preparation for a drink requires such an amount of time and trouble that, when a chief once gets his lips to the liquid, he drinks enough to last him a considerable time.

With respect to actual knowledge of medicine and surgery, these charm-doctors sometimes display great skill, more especially in the extraction of bullets. A man has, perhaps, several slugs shot into him ; some of them more or less jagged, and generally deeply embedded, for a native rarely fires unless he is very close upon his enemy. The wounded man is firmly held by the arms and legs, and the medicine-man, literally smothered in his " charm " paraphernalia, and always with a grave countenance, as if he had some weighty matter upon his mind, and seeming to be afraid of lessening his own importance by intercourse with ordinary human beings, compels everybody around to sit down, and allows no one to stand behind him. Procuring a basin of water, he puts in a shell or two, to charm it, and, taking a stiff hair of an elephant's tail, he probes the wound, finding out exactly where

the bullet is.   Then, by squeezing and pinching the flesh, he
gradually brings the slug near the surface.   He then crunches

leaves in his hands,
until, rendering them
soft and spongy, he
places over each wound
a little bunch of these
bruised leaves, and
then renews his opera-
tions until he feels that
the slug is out.   In
order to convey an
impression of mys-
tery to the operation,
he confers with his
charms, puts different-
colored powders on
the wounded man,
and, after gesticula-
ting with a little idol,
finally pronounces to
the assembly that the
slug has been charmed
to the surface.   He
will then pick it off
the mouth of the
wound, and drop it
into the basin of water,

A BANKUNDU FAMILY.

and so on, until he has extracted every bullet, varying the pan-
tomime which accompanies the dislodgment of each slug from
the wound.

One of the most important positions on the Congo is that of Bakute, in which district is situated the " Station of the Equator," so called from its geographical position. Surrounded, as it is, by powerful cannibal tribes, and being the center of an important river system, it forms a convenient base for exploring operations, either scientific or commercial.

The actual natives of the soil are the Bankundu people, a branch of the great Lolo race. They are not very keen traders confining themselves to hunting and fishing. There is, however, a little colony of the Babangi people who have settled amongst them for the purpose of trade. There are several large inland villages, the most important of which is that of Monsolé, situated about twenty miles back from the Congo River. The government of this village differs altogether from that generally met with. As a rule, a village is split up into small communities, each acknowledging its respective chief ; but in this particular instance, the whole district acknowledges but one chief, " Euelu," who has gained this position by his courage and prowess in war. His name is feared by all the surrounding villages. In stature this man is small, but strongly built, with a face, although savage, denoting a very strong will.

There are, of course, several minor chiefs in the district, but they all acknowledge him as their head, and he reserves to himself alone the right of waging war, and draws upon any part of the district for his warriors. A visit to this village will at once convince the traveler that intelligence far superior to that of the ordinary native has been at work. The houses are built in two parallel lines, with a large, open, well kept street between them. Immediately at the back of these houses, the ground has been cleared, and banana-trees planted at such a distance apart as to afford no cover to an approaching enemy. In any weak part of the village, where an attack from a hostile tribe would probably be made, rough but effective stockades have been built. The security that these people were enjoying at the time of which I am writing, was shown by their general prosperity and content-ment. As there is always a fear of intertribal wars, the inhabit-ants never think it worth while to build good houses or raise any stock, fearing that any moment their houses may be burned and all their belongings stolen. But the people of Monsolé had no such fear and, therefore, bestowed a great deal of attention upon rais-ing goats and fowls, and, moreover, took great pride in building good houses and having their village clean and tidy.

Euelu was very aggressive and took great delight in subjecting the surrounding villages to his sway. But his repeated wars cost the lives of many of his own people, and in the spring of '89 such dissatisfaction was felt with his policy that he was waylaid and brutally murdered.

In the neighborhood of Monsolé is a settlement of the Barumbe, a nomadic tribe of native hunters. In former times these people were in the habit of visiting this district periodically, stopping for six and eight months, during which time they would hunt the wild boar and antelope, exchanging the meat with the neighboring villages for beads and different kinds of trinkets ; but Euelu saw the advantage of having such a useful community in the vicinity of his village, and, upon his suggestion, the Barumbe have now become settled. They are people of a very low caste, so much so that they are not allowed to intermarry with the Monsolé. Their type of head stamps them as an inferior race. However, they are very industrious and inoffensive, and have now quite resigned themselves to their settled life ; extensive plantations of manioc,

A BAKUTE VILLAGE.

peanuts, and other vegetables have sprung up around their villages. The men still carry on their occupation as hunters, making excursions into the surrounding country for two or three days at a time, killing the smaller animals with their bows and arrows. They then smoke or dry the meat, and carry it around to the neighboring villages for sale. By this means some have become wealthy, from a native point of view, and they are now the possessors of several slaves. The Barumbe have lived so long in the forests, and have had such opportunities of studying animal life, that the habits of every bird and animal are well known to them. There is also in their favor the fact that they are not cannibals, as are the Monsolé; neither do they make human sacrifices at the death of a chief.

Since the death of Euelu, no man has been found capable of replacing him as chief of the whole district, and the population is now split up into several parties, each acknowledging a separate chief. Disputes have sprung up, and intertribal wars amongst the Monsolé are continually taking place, and the power of this once universally feared tribe is now on the wane. The Monsolé are cannibals, but they confine themselves generally to eating enemies slain in battle,

CHAPTER II.

THREE GREAT TRIBUTARIES TO THE CONGO—THE BALUI HUNTERS OF THE HIPPOPOTAMI—
THE TRIBAL MARKS—SKULLS OF VICTIMS TO CANNIBALISM—WEIRD DECORATION—
VAST FOREST SWAMPS—NATIVE MODE OF ELEPHANT HUNTING—VILLAGES ON PILES

THERE are three large rivers, besides several small ones, which empty themselves into the Congo, in the vicinity of the Equator Station : namely, the Ruki, Lulungu and Oubangi. The last-mentioned river enters the Congo on the north bank, nearly oppo-site Bakute, and is navigable for four hundred miles, until the Zongo rapids are reached. It is, without doubt, identical with Schweinfurth's Quelle, as the customs of the people inhabiting these two rivers coincide exactly. But although the upper reaches of the Oubangi have been explored, yet, as no scientific observations were taken, the problem still remains unsolved to the geographical world.

The lower reaches of this river are inhabited by the Balui, a branch of the dreaded Bangalas ; and who, like their parent tribe, are great cannibals, and cause much bloodshed by the piratical expeditions which they make upon neighboring and weaker people. They are keen hunters, and display great intelligence in making traps to kill all kinds of game found in their forests. There are numerous herds of hippopotami at the mouth of this river, which the Balui hunt in canoes.

At noon, when the sun is hot, two Balui hunters, having found a sleeping hippopotamus in a suitable position, will approach noiselessly, handling their paddles so carefully that no splash is heard. Then one of the men takes a spear and plunges it into the body of the unconscious brute, the other man standing ready to paddle off with all his might to escape the fury of the wounded monster. To the spear is attached a cord, on the end of which is fastened a small block of light wood, so that, by the means of this float, the whereabouts of the wounded animal are always known to the natives. As he plunges about in the water, maddened by pain, he is followed at a respectful distance by the hunters, until, having succumbed to his wounds, he comes to the surface dead, and is towed into some shallow water, and is cut up. Many of these men lose their lives in this dangerous occupation, as they are very often perceived by the brute before they have time to get away; then the canoe is capsized, and the occupants are soon mangled to death by the irate animal.

Higher up the river are found the M'Bunju, who speak quite a different language, and are of a different type, resembling the Balui only in ferocity and cannibalism. They are not distinguishable by any special kind of cicatrization, but have the habit of cutting out their two front teeth, and piercing their ears, in which they wear rings of an enormous size, made of wire, ivory, and sometimes of wood. Their mode of hair-dressing is peculiar to themselves. They completely shave the head, and then allow the hair to grow all over for three or four weeks, after which they shave designs, such as half-moons, stars, squares, and parallel lines. When the hair grows too long for the design to be visible, the whole scalp is again shaved, and some different pattern adopted. The people are as voracious cannibals as any tribe in the Congo Free States.

A chief's position is esteemed according to the number of slaves he is able to kill. The skulls of the victims to cannibalism are always exposed in some prominent position in the village, as a mark of the importance of the chief. Sometimes a house will be decorated with human skulls placed in rows, on small platforms built for the purpose, on the four sides of the house. In other places the skulls are hung about in bunches on poles. From chairs and even drinking horns, attached by cords, will often be seen three or four human jaw-bones.

Along this river every village seems to be continually at war with its neighbors, so that great precautions are taken to guard against surprise. Stockades of sharpened poles surround nearly every village, and a deep dike is dug just outside this barrier, the only entrance to the village being by means of a small draw-bridge in the shape of a single tree slung across the trench, which, at night, and in time of danger, is taken away. Such a fortification, defended by a handful of resolute men, would be impregnable to the attacks of native raiders. The natives generally obtain their victims on the river. They are continually prowling about in their large war-canoes, making excursions to parts known to be frequented by small bands of hunters and fishermen, who are easily vanquished, bound, and, in due course, killed and eaten.

The mouth of the Oubangi is a delta of small, swampy forest and grass islands, which form a most convenient hunting ground for the piratical Balui, who raid in their canoes, and, armed to the teeth, lie in wait, concealed by the thick, overhanging vegetation ; and any canoe containing a weaker force than their own, upon being sighted, is immediately given chase to, some of the occupants being speared, and others caught and taken into slavery, there to be fed up and slaughtered at the next cannibal orgy.

The nature of the land through which the Oubangi flows is exceedingly swampy : it is only here and there that patches of high ground are found, and they are invariably inhabited. The banks of the river are lined by the most luxuriant forest vegetation, broken occasionally by large grass plains, the home of numerous herds of buffaloes and antelopes. There is a great deal of elephant ivory in this country, but at present the natives will only sell their ivory for human slaves, and no offer of beads, cowries, brass bells or any other kind of trinket will tempt them. They are people of very fine physique, and are industrious, spending their time principally in hunting and fishing.

A TYPE OF BOLOBO.

Above the rapids of the Zongo is said to be a country rich in ivory, and with a numerous population, and there is every appearance of the Oubangi river becoming, when the country is opened up, the richest affluent of the Congo.

Just above, and on the same side as the Equator Station, the Ruki river empties into the Congo.

As yet little is known concerning the habits and customs of the people living on the banks of this river. In no other part of the Congo has the white traveler had so much difficulty in convincing the natives of his good intentions. The general reception accorded strangers at the hands of these people is a flight of arrows; and even after they have been bartering their fowls, food of different kinds, and weapons, in exchange for beads and other trinkets, they will signalize the departure of the boat from their beach by a flight of arrows and insulting cries. The bow and arrow is their sole weapon, and they are very expert in the use of it. Some of their arrows have iron barbed heads, whilst others, far more dangerous, are simply strips made of split bamboo cane about twelve inches long, sharpened to a point, and smeared with deadly poison. The inhabitants of this river are Bankundu, and can only be distinguished from those at the equator by a slight variation in their cicatrization. They are voracious cannibals, a fact which they do not disguise.

The banks of this river are in places low-lying and swampy. Still a great deal of high land is found always covered with thick vegetation, or dotted with the villages of the inhabitants. The Ruki is a fine, deep stream with a strong current; its water being of a dark hue, the contrast in color between it and the Congo is very discernible at its mouth.

There are large herds of elephants and buffaloes on both sides of the river, which are hunted by the more inland tribes, and the ivory sold to the dwellers upon the banks of the river. These hunters build platforms up in the trees, out of reach of an elephant's trunk.

Hundreds of such platforms are erected in various parts of the woods, the places selected being, of course, those where herds of elephants are known to pass through on their way to their feeding-grounds, or are attracted by a plentiful supply of water in the neighborhood. When news is brought in that there are elephants in a wood which has been so prepared, the natives hasten to get into positions on these platforms, armed with their deadly spears. They generally try to drive their spears between the shoulders of the brute, and, as a rule, they manage to pick out two or three amongst a herd which passes near enough to the platforms to come within effective range of their weapons.

Sometimes they will attack an elephant on foot. This is indeed a very plucky and hazardous thing to do.

They stealthily crawl up alongside the elephant, armed only with a spear which has a broad, sharp blade attached to a long, thick handle. Upon getting near enough to their ponderous game, they either spear him in the groin, or ham-string him. Holding, with both hands, the haft of the spear, they thrust the blade in with all their might, and, as a rule, they manage to bring the beast down on the spot, or to wound him

A TYPE OF BALOLO.

so severely that they are able to track him, by the blood marks, to his retreat, where they finish him off. Of course, as soon as they have delivered their blow they make off, to escape the fury of the wounded animal, and the nature of the ground, covered as it is with large, thick-trunked trees, enables them to dodge his movements or take to the shelter of the branches.

From a commercial point of view, the richest affluent of the

Congo, as yet known, is certainly the Lulungu, whose mouth, where it empties into the Congo, is situated a few miles above the Ruki. The Lulungu is formed by the confluence of two rivers, the Malinga and Lopori, which, uniting at the populous village of Massankusu, from that point form a stream a mile in width, and probably one hundred and fifty miles in length, until its waters are swallowed up in those of the mighty Congo. The lower stretch of river is inhabited by Bankundu ivory and slave traders; the upper reaches, as far as the swamps around the headwaters of the Malinga and Lopori, by the Balolo proper, and rude tribes of elephant hunters, who store their ivory until the periodical visits of the down-river

A FISH SPEARER.

traders, when they exchange it for beads, cowries and brass ornaments.

These Baiolo tribes are an oppressed and persecuted people.
Timid and inoffensive, they fall an easy prey to the overwhelming numbers of the powerful inland tribes of the Lufembe and
Ngombe, who are continually making raids upon them, capturing
and selling them into slavery, and eating those who are less
suitable for the slavemarket.

The Lulungu and its two great feeders, particularly the
Malinga, flow through a swampy country, the greater part of the
land during the rainy season being under water.

So swampy is it, that all the native villages on the upper reaches
of that river are built on piles standing in water from two to four
feet in depth. It is a strange sight, when the water is high, to
see all these houses dotted about on the river, looking like floating boxes, and it is comical to observe a native fishing from his
tiny veranda, or when he wishes to pay a visit to a friend across
the way, or journey to another part of the village, to see him step
into his canoe from off his doorstep, and paddle about the streets
of swiftly running water.

Ivory is hidden for safety in the water under their houses, or
at some point of the forest known only to the owner, where the
long tree-trunks stand up out of the brown, dark-shadowed flood
of the swollen river, and, should he wish to sell it, he must dive
for it.

The effect seen from the river of one of these villages is very
striking. Large trees are felled all about, so as to render the
progress of an approaching canoe difficult. These wretched houses,
without walls, and with a fire made on a flat lump of clay, or a
platform formed by cross-sticks, form indeed wretched habitations

for human beings. You will see on some prominent position a large war-drum, so that in case of an attack, or any danger arising, the surrounding villages may be signaled, and timely warning given.

The natives living in these watery settlements say that inland they can find strips and patches of dry land, but that if they live there, the slave-raiders find out their whereabouts, and continually persecute them, so that, inconvenient and wretched as it is living in houses on piles, yet they naturally prefer it to the danger of slavery and death. However, they are not free from molestation even under these circumstances, as the slave-raiders from the lower reaches of the river form large expeditions, sometimes of two hundred and three hundred canoes, well-armed, and go up and kill, catch, and take them into slavery.

CHAPTER III.

IN '77, when within a thousand miles of the Atlantic Ocean, on his marvelous journey through the Dark Continent, Mr. Stanley was attacked by the warlike Bangalas, a tribe numbering upward of thirty thousand savage cannibals, whose villages were situated along the north bank of the Congo, under the shade of beautiful palm forests, and thickly fringed with long lines of plantain and banana trees.

They manned their great war-canoes, and charged time after time into Stanley's little flotilla, and it was only by dint of hard fighting, and the superiority of their arms, that Stanley and his band of faithful followers were able to repel their fierce antagonists. For hundreds of miles he had already run the gauntlet of attacks such as these ; and the cries of " niama, niama "—" meat, meat "—with which the savages pursued him, too plainly revealed the nature of the fate which awaited him and his companions, should they falls into the hands of their assailants.

It will be remembered that after Stanley's return to civilization, great interest was aroused throughout the whole civilized world, by the story of what he had seen in the vast unexplored regions of the Congo valley—a territory which covers so many hundred thousand square miles of equatorial Africa. Hitherto it had been believed that Central Africa was but a counterpart of the Sahara—an unpeopled waste of arid desert, absolutely impenetrable to the white man, and incapable of rewarding the toil and difficulties attendant upon all attempts at exploration.

Mr. Stanley told to the world another tale ; and, moved by the story of the great explorer, and actuated by the highest motives of patriotism and a desire to benefit others besides his own countrymen—to give to the poor savages of the Congo the means of coming in contact with the enlightened influences of civilization, as well as to find another outlet for the products and energies of the white man, His Majesty King Leopold II., of the Belgians, commissioned Mr. Stanley to return to the scene of his explorations at the head of a well equipped expedition, and to undertake the work of founding stations along the course of the Congo, which should prove the means of opening up that great highway to the advance of commerce, and of winning the tribes along its banks to a condition of peaceful industry, and a desire to obtain the benefits they beheld the white men possessing in their midst.

This work Mr. Stanley initiated with rare skill and intrepid perseverance, and ere abandoning the scene of his labors in 1884, after having founded stations along the Congo for 1500 miles and negotiated numerous treaties with the savage chiefs throughout the country, by which they bound themselves to recognize the authority of these stations and to assist the work of peace and progress, he had the satisfaction of beholding his labors crowned with success, and the gratification of having created the Congo Free State, which, in 1885, received the recognition of the civilized powers of the world.

It was to one of these stations, that of Bangala, situated in the heart of the populous district inhabited by the tribe of that name, I found myself appointed in the year 1886.

BLOOD BROTHERHOOD.

The paramount chief of the Bangalas at that time was Mata Bwiki, or more correctly, Mata Mwiki, meaning "many guns," a title bestowed upon him in deference to the number of flint-lock guns he and his followers possessed. He was a man of probably sixty years of age, nearly six feet in height, with massive shoulders and big bones, and his countenance was rendered more cruel than it otherwise would have been, by the loss of an eye.

The Bangalas originally belonged to the tribe of Mobeka, which resides 150 miles higher up the river ; but about forty years ago, Mata Bwiki gathered around him some enterprising young bloods, and commenced a series of marauding expeditions through the surrounding country. So successful were these excursions, that Mata Bwiki was able to establish himself at Iboko, where the tribe has increased and flourished ever since, and is widely known by the name of Bangala or "People of the Ngala."

Among my first experiences after taking command of the station was that of submitting myself to the ceremony of blood-brotherhood with Mata Bwiki ; a form of cementing friendship and a guarantee of good faith, popular with all Upper Congo tribes.

In the presence of hundreds of the savages owning the sway of Mata Bwiki, we were seated upon the low wooden stools placed opposite each other. Silence being commanded by the beating of the big redwood drums, which give forth a hollow sound that can be heard for miles, a charm-doctor appeared, arrayed in all his mystic apparel. An incision was made in both our right arms, in the outer muscular swelling just below the elbow, and as the blood flowed in a tiny stream, the charm-doctor sprinkled powdered chalk and potash on the wounds, delivering the while, in rapid tones, an appeal to us to maintain unbroken the sanctity of the contract; and then our arms being rubbed together, so that the flowing blood intermingled, we were declared to be brothers of one blood, whose interests henceforth should be united as our blood now was. The witnesses of this strange ceremony expressed their agreement with the utterances of the charm-doctor, and gave way to boisterous expressions of approval of what had been done already, ere setting to work to drink the huge earthenware jars of fermented juice of the sugar-cane, known as "masanga," which had previously been prepared to celebrate the event.

From my position as commander of the fortified station in their midst, as well as from my desire to be on the friendliest terms with the natives, I was able to see a good deal of their modes of life, and of the "interior economy" of the arrange-ments among the Bangalas.

Almost weekly some savage act of cannibalism would be brought to my notice, and, although the villagers in the imme-diate vicinity of the station did, after a time, become chary of acknowledging to a white man their liking for human flesh, or their participation in these orgies, I knew that I should never have far to seek to find my friends of to-day, with old Mata Bwiki at their head, indulging in a light repast off the limbs of some unfortunate slave, slain for refractory behavior, or banqueting upon the bodies of the enemies slaughtered in some recent con-flict.

All was flesh that came to their net ; and if a slave, captured in war, or sold into bondage by a neighboring people, became "uppish" and discontented with his walk in life, the remedy was simple. They no longer 'troubled him to continue treading a path which proved a weariness to the flesh. The pot became his

destination, and he soon
ceased to afford even a
topic for conversation.
This may seem incredi-
ble, and yet I have an
instance in my mind's
eye of such an occur-
rence having actually
taken place at Bangala
only one year ago.

A slave boy had been
permitted to engage him-
self to work on the sta-
tion of the agent, at
Bangala, of the Belgian
Trading Company. Af-
ter a time, he absented
himself during working
hours, without the per-
mission of the agent,
who complained to the
boy's master, a small
chief in the neighboring
village, informing him
at the same time that
the boy was a lazy fel-
low and not worth much.
A day or two later the
chief told the trader,
with evident satisfac-

BANGALA GIRL.

tion, that the boy would not trouble him again, for that he had killed him with a thrust of his spear ; and the white man's horror was increased when, on the following day, the chief's son, a youngster of sixteen or seventeen years of age, came swaggering into the station with spear and shield, and nonchalantly remarked that—

"That slave boy was very good eating—he was nice and fat."

Notwithstanding their cannibal propensities, our relations with the natives of the various villages comprising the Bangala district, were, as a rule, friendly. The garrison of the State station consisted of Zanzibaris and Houssas, men of a Mahommedan tribe on the Upper Niger, engaged by agents of the government on that river or at the gold-coast port of Lagos, for a term of three years, and conveyed to the Congo by the mail steamers.

These men were brave and warlike ; but, lacking in the cunning and readiness of resource, characteristic of the savage, and, at times, by the very stupidity of their valor, they fell an easy prey to the Bangalas in the attacks made upon the stations consequent upon a rupture of our friendly intercourse with the natives. On one occasion, during a misunderstanding which had grown into a conflict between garrison and natives, an attack upon the outworks of the station had been delivered by the Bangalas, who, as usual, were beaten back by the rifle fire, when the Houssas, issuing from the cover of their walls, penetrated into the long grass and bush through which the enemy had retreated, in search of foes or plunder. Two of them, following up one of the many tracks through the high, overhanging grass, in pursuit of flying enemies, had their careers brought to an untimely end by the stroke of a knife delivered from the cover of the grass on their unprotected necks. The sharp weapon, wielded, no doubt, by a skillful hand, had severed the heads completely from the bodies, and later in the day their corpses and the ghastly heads of the two

MOLANGI, A BANGALA CHIEFTAIN

poor fellows were discovered by their comrades after the Bangala attack had been completely beaten off.

Often the savages will feign to fly, knowing the propensity of the Houssas to pursue, heedless of ambuscade; and to stimulate

them to scatter through the grass and banana groves, goats and
fowls, bleating and cackling, will be tied up as decoys in proximity
to the line of retreat, near which bands of armed men station
themselves to greet the would-be spoilers with a welcome they
little expected.   Some months of apprenticeship to this species of
guerrilla warfare rendered the Houssa soldiers more fit to cope
with the wily Bangala upon his own ground.

The white men who have successively held the post of Commander of Bangala Station, have endeavored, and with some
success, to repress the practice of eating human flesh in the districts around the station, but in the remoter villages of the settlement cannibalism is still openly indulged in, and a man will boast
of the number of enemies he has devoured, hang their bleached
and whitened skulls from a tree by his doorway, or arrange them
in line on the roof-tree of his house as silent testimonies of his
importance and valor.

It is customary among the Upper Congo people to stamp their
features and persons, by means of cicatrization, with various
designs, differing according to the tribe.   About the age of four
the operation is first commenced, the skin of the face being
gashed in conformity with the tribal pattern ; after some months
have elapsed, so that the wounds may be completely healed, they
are re-cut, and each gash is filled with redwood powder, produced
from crushed camwood, of which the forest yields a plentiful supply.   After frequent repetitions of this barbarous mutilation, the
skin and flesh becomes hardened and protrude in lumps, between
the incisions.

In my drawings, the effects of this mode of marking the face
are illustrated.

The Bangala tribal mark consists of a series of horizontal

cross-cuts half an inch in length, extending down the center of the forehead from the hair to between the eyes, with a smaller patch of diagonal cuts upon the temples.

That of the Balolo or "Iron People," a numerous race inhabiting the banks of the Lulungu or Malinga and Ruki rivers, the two great tributaries which empty into the Congo on the southern bank, is formed by the creation of three separate lumps, as large as and similar in shape to pigeons' eggs—one either on the bridge of the nose or higher up toward the centre of the forehead, with the others flanking it upon each temple. Occasionally, to these will be added, as a sort of a pendant, or, perhaps, to compensate, yet a fourth upon the chin,

WIFE OF MOLANGI.

while the bodies of the happy possessors of this uncouth adornment, particularly those of the women, will be covered with a series of lumps standing out darkly from the paler skin, which thus adorned, might very well serve for a map of the midnight sky.

Indeed, I have seen one stout Lolo lady who sported an entire solar system upon her back, and might have told off all the stars in the milky way, with an equal number of excrescences upon her stately bust, and, even then, have had a few handfuls to spare scattered down her legs, to pit against the nebulæ forming the limbs of Andromeda.

Others again, and notable among them are the Bateke, whom I have already mentioned as inhabiting the shores of Stanley Pool, and the northwestern bank of the Congo, from that point up to near the confluence of the Oubangi River, score their cheeks and temples with long, thin incisions, much resembling the cuts made by a butcher upon a piece of pork to tempt the would-be purchaser with visions of " crackling."

The Bateke around Stanley Pool are not known to practice cannibalism, although they have been suspected more than once, recently, when celebrating the funeral ceremonies of some chieftains in the neighborhood of Ndolo and Mfwa, on the north bank, of having had recourse to other baked meats than those which legitimate mourning prescribes for such occasions.   Their cousins, the Apfouru upon the Alima, and kindred Bateke tribes in the French territories of the Congo basin, must, I fear, be classed among the cannibals of the Congo ; although to what extent the revolting custom prevails among them is unknown.

The Balolo, strange to say, are not united in their desire of eating human flesh : for, while upon the Ruki River they are known to be anthropophagi, and by personal observation of white men who have journeyed up the long, swampy stretches of the Malinga, have been identified on portions of that river with the same practice, yet, at other spots, no traces of cannibalism have been discovered among them ; and, on being questioned, they have denied all participation in such practices.

Such a denial, accompanied by the softer manners and gentler appearance of the people making it, to those of the known cannibals lower down the river, convinced those who have visited their villages of the truth of the assertion ; for this being the first time white men had ever gone among these people, or put such a question to them, they had no reason in concealing the fact of their cannibalism (if it were a fact), since they could not then have known or conceived the abhorrence with which the white man regards that practice. It must not be supposed, however, that the cannibal tribes of the interior are altogether brutal in every action of life. On the contrary, I have observed more frequent traits of affection for wife and children among them than are exhibited in the conduct of domestic affairs among the people of the lower, or Ba Congo country, who are not cannibals, nor addicted to the shedding of blood, save in religious matters.

A native of the upper river will embrace his wife ere he sets out on a fighting expedition, or will fondle his child, and even condescend to give the infant its morning bath in the river if the mother be unable to perform that act ; but during all my stay among the Ba Congo, I only once observed a father kiss his child ; and I have never witnessed any display of tenderness betwixt man and wife.

On one occasion I happened to be journeying from Stanley Pool to Boma, the seat of government, along with a party of eighty or one hundred Bangala men who had been recruited to act as soldiers on the lower river, and were now traveling to their destination. Probably twenty women accompanied the party, wives of the head men ; they were all toiling painfully along the hilly road, unaccustomed to so much walking or such hard roads in their own swampy country. After five days' weary marching our path led us to the fords of the Luasa River, through whose swollen waters, running now breast high, we had to wade.

The party crossed without much difficulty beyond a wetting of the bare skin, but the force of the current was such that the fatigued women found trouble in keeping their feet, and battling their way across. One very young and frail-looking girl feared to enter the stream and stood hesitating on the nearer bank, when her husband, a strapping young fellow of twenty-five or so, seeing her anxiety, turned back from the point he had reached in the water, and, tenderly gathering her up in his arms, placed her upon his shoulder. Thus burdened, he stepped again into the river and bore her safely to the other side, the girl clinging to his head and neck the while with every mark of confidence and affection.

CHAPTER IV.

REFLECTIONS—A RIVER SCENE—"A WANDERING MINSTREL, I"—MASANGA AND ITS RESULTS—A WOUNDED SAVAGE—MATA BWIKI QUELLS A DISTURBANCE.

SOME Bakongo carriers who witnessed this display of kindness toward a woman by a man-eating savage, having never been guilty themselves of a similar action, were lost in wonder and then laughingly remarked to one another that their wives would be a long time standing on the bank of a stream before they should catch them rendering a like service. And yet the Bangala man probably had more than once pronounced a critical opinion upon the flavor of an enemy, while the scoffers at marital affection would shudder at the mere mention of eating human flesh.

I find it strange to myself when I think over the many conflicting emotions I have often observed betraying themselves in the lives of these savages ; swayed one moment by a thirst for blood and indulging in the most horrible orgies, they may yet the next be found approaching their homes looking forward with the liveliest interest to the caresses of their wives and children, or, with patient gaze regarding the strange surroundings of the white man, in his mud-built house, and listening politely to his uncouth and ridiculous attempts at expressing himself in their language, assisting him with a word when he hesitates, and supplying the many gaps in the sense of his utterances by a timely smile of encouragement or a hopeless effort to render his meaning clear to the other listening ears. Such little gatherings, when spear and shield are laid aside at the doorway, and young and old congregate in the shade of the rough veranda, to listen to the words of wisdom that falteringly fall from the white man's lips, after he has accepted the presents of fowls and bananas, or "malafu" (palm wine) in dark earthen jars brought by the leaders of the assembled guests, form the pleasantest recollections of my life on the Upper Congo.

All is serene and calm ; canoes with fishermen, or hunters returning from the chase of the wild pig in the woods of the larger islands, glide noiselessly in and out of the deeply shaded channels. The silence that reigns everywhere is unbroken until at first faintly from the distance, and then swelling louder, the rich, wild song of a party of ivory traders coming home from Usindi or Lulanga, their big canoes gay with piles of red cloth topped with wide-opened parti-colored umbrellas, as the paddlers bend their strong backs to every stroke, and the spray is cast behind in glistening showers, floats into the sheltered veranda, and mingles with the hum of laughing, talking voices that fill the room ; the blue sky and bright sunlight without, seemingly made to light up the bronzed features and rows of white teeth of the women carrying water from the river past the open door to the village—all combine to make up a scene of peaceful beauty that powerfully influences the mind of the beholder, and insensibly the white man, gazing on the good-tempered and smiling faces around him, forgets the cannibalism and cruelty that too often have darkened them; forgets, too, his distant home with its cold, gray sky ; and feels for the moment one in sympathy and accord with the human beings who surround him.

An American organette, the scanty stock of music for which consisted of a few much damaged sheets of marches and opera-

comique airs, played an important part in these meetings ; and when conversation
flagged, or the malafu cup
circled less freely, I would be
called upon to oblige the
company by giving a selec-
tion on this instrument. One
man, Lolo, named Injiolama,
liked only the waltz tune, "A
Wandering Minstrel, I," from
Gilbert and Sullivan's "Mik-
ado," and repeatedly he would
visit me in the morning, and,
asking me to pick out the
circular sheet of that piece of
music and arrange it on the
organ, he would turn the
handle and churn out "A
Wandering Minstrel, I," until
I had every reason to regret
that he had discovered the
power of music to charm the
savage breast.

But the harmony of this
existence was often rudely
interrupted.

Strolling through the
native village one afternoon
with my sketch book, I

BANGALA SLAVE GIRL.

found two or three hundred men and women seated around a large earthenware pot of fermented sugar-cane juice, known as "masanga." An evil-looking, broad shouldered savage was seated, distributing the potent beverage with a long-handled ladle. Spears lay on the ground beside each man, and many of the women were sitting cross-legged on the war-shields, which are made of basket-work, and ornamented with black stains of various devices. As I scrutinized the group, with a view to selecting a good type to draw, there was a sound in the distance of angry altercation, which interrupted the drinking, and caused all to listen. As the noise of angry voices increased, each man reached down by his side, gathering up his spears, and simultaneously they rushed away in the direction of the brawl, followed by the women, who cried and wrung their hands, and besought their husbands to remain. Soon I was left alone with the overturned stools and the half-empty masanga pot. Not wishing to witness the scene of bloodshed that I knew was about to take place, I sat down and commenced sketching the various shapes of the natives chairs. In the distance the roar of voices increased, and every now and then I could hear the piercing shrieks of women, which betokened the wounding of husband or friend. Gradually the sound of angry voices abated, and only the laments of the women filled the air. Occasionally I heard a gruff voice delivering a short, defiant speech; then I caught sight of the returning rabble. The big, burly savage, who had previously presided over the masanga pot, staggered along in front of the others; his feather head-dress hung drooping on one shoulder, and he dragged his great spear along the ground by the haft. He stood silent in front of me for awhile, grinding his teeth, his body swaying from weakness and exhaustion. He said : +

"A GAPING WOUND IN HIS LEFT SHOULDER FROM WHICH THE BLOOD FLOWED COPIOUSLY."

"Keka, Nkumbe"—"Look, Black Hawk," ("Nkumbe,"—
"Black Hawk," was my native name among the Bangala tribe),
and he pointed to a gaping wound in his left shoulder, from which
the blood flowed copiously. His weeping women approached and
tried to embrace him; one woman threw herself on the ground
and encircled his knees with her arms, crying piteously. He several times roughly shook them off, and at last, impatient, he brutally swung his spear around, inflicting deep flesh wounds upon
several of the poor women.

It was an impressive sight to watch his gigantic figure trem-
bling with pain, his head drooping on his chest, covered with blood
and dust, not deigning to speak, so full was he of suppressed rage.
He grated his teeth, as every now and then he scowled upon the
frightened women, who were moaning and sobbing in each other's
arms.

Returning home, my path led through the village in which the
dispute had taken place, and I was horrified to see a further and
more ghastly evidence of the fray. There were lying the bodies
of two men who had been speared to death.

The dispute which led to this sanguinary result arose from the
simple fact that one native had used another's canoe without permission. The rightful owner claimed some slight payment, which
was refused. Angry words were succeeded by blows, when they
were joined by the other savages, who, semi-intoxicated and excited,
were but too anxious for a fight. It was only after two men had
been killed and several wounded, that the old chief, Mata Bwiki
was able to quell the disturbance.

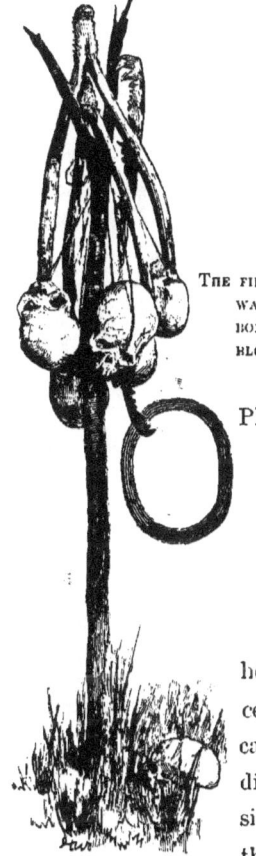

CHAPTER V.

The FIRST WHITE MAN TO VISIT MOBUNGA—"WHAT DO YOU WANT? WAR?" — SAVAGES SOOTHED BY A MUSICAL BOX—"MASTER WAKE UP AND GET YOUR GUN"—A BLOODY DEED.

PPOSITE the Bangalas, on the other side of the Congo River, there is a populous village, known as Mobunga. The people are of an inferior type to the Bangalas, and their countenances clearly denote their brutal, savage natures.

When I first heard that there were herds of elephants in this country, I proceeded across the river in a large war canoe, accompanied by two Houssa soldiers, natives from the English possessions of the west coast of Africa, and thirty-five Bangala natives.

Great excitement attended my appearance ; for the natives had never before been visited by a white man. They crowded in hundreds along the river bank as we approached, refusing, at first, to allow us to land, when the old chief forced his way through the throng, and, commanding silence by the wave of his hand, said in a loud tone to me : "Benu Bokuling unde, Itumba ?" ("What do

"WHAT DO YOU WANT? WAH?"

you want, war?") I then explained to him that we came as
friends, that the Bangala had told me of the large herds of
elephants that roamed through the forests of his country, that I
came with my gun to shoot elephants, that a portion of the meat
of the elephants I shot should belong to them, and that I desired
to camp in his village.

He replied, amidst a breathless silence of the assembled savages,
that I could come in his village with my two Houssa soldiers, but
that the Bangalas must remain on the river bank. For, should
they be permitted in the village, trouble and bloodshed might
ensue from the raking up of old tribal feuds. He also added that
I must become a blood brother with him, in evidence of my good
faith. I acceded to this arrangement, and, in order to prevent
trouble, I sent my Bangalas away in the canoe back to their own
village, with instructions to return for me after four days.

For several hours, until sunset, I was surrounded by numbers
of inquisitive, foul smelling savages, whose black, beady eyes
watched keenly my every movement. The ceremony of blood-
brotherhood was similar to the ordeal I passed through with Mata
Bwiki, the big chief of Bangala.

In order to divert the attention of the boisterous multitude, I
ordered Alakai, one of my Houssa soldiers, to turn the handle of
the little musical box that I invariably carried with me. It was
advertised to play one tune, " Home, Sweet Home;" but, in consequence of hard knocks and the damp and enervating influence
of the African climate, the beautiful air was rendered almost
indistinguishable. The savages, however, listened with delight to
the tinkling of the little instrument, nudging one another, and gazed
at the wonder-working instrument with widely opened eyes, as, in
astonishment and delight, they covered their open mouths with

their hands. The innate love of music was aroused within them, and their bodies swayed, serpent-like, in cadence with the tune.

Shortly after sunset, I was left with my two Houssa soldiers, in a dilapidated old grass hut, without walls. I arranged my blankets and mosquito curtain, and, after a frugal supper of maize and bananas, I lay down to sleep.

Having posted the Houssas as sentries on either side of my little grass shelter, I slept fitfully until about midnight, when I was aroused by Alakai's black head appearing through my mos-quito curtain.

" Master, master, wake up and get your gun !" said he, in a hoarse whisper.

In an instant I was on my feet, and could see, occasionally, the gleam of spear-heads amidst the thick foliage of banana trees, plantations of which extended on both sides of my hut.

We quietly arranged our ammunition and guns ready for an attack. It was hopeless to think of escape, for we were fully a mile from the river bank. I realized our position keenly, as I strained my ears to catch every little sound that would betoken their movements. We were three against many thousands. There could be no help for us, and we awaited our doom. Every moment we expected the savages to swoop down upon us with a yell. We felt one consolation, however, and that was our ability to sell our lives dearly ; for we had good rifles, whilst the natives were only armed with knives and spears. The time passed slowly, but still we continued unmolested. All was silent, except every now and again we could hear hoarse whispers among the natives, who were congregated in the shadow of the graceful banana leaves. Suddenly we heard in the distance a roar of angry voices, growing rapidly nearer to us ; then a sound of footsteps rushing toward us, and in another moment, we saw three or four dusky forms fleeing past, followed by a rabble of armed men, whose spears and knives glistened in the bright moonlight, whose feather head-dresses fluttered as they ran, and whose heavy iron anklets and bracelets clanked and clashed as they tore along after their prey. They were joined by the people who had been previously hiding among the banana trees, and gradually the sound of the uproar grew fainter in the distance, until it culminated in piercing screams and groans. Then we were electrified by a shrill shriek of despair, and all was still, except the low muttering of voices in the distance, which gradually increased as they returned toward us. What could this mean? We waited breathlessly, our guns in hand, ready for any emergency. The rabble took another road on their return, and, in the uncertain light, we caught sight of at least two hundred armed men as they filed past by a small path in the distance. The tone of their voices suggested satisfaction. Occasionally I could hear a brutal laugh, and then some young blood would mimic the shrieks which we heard. The noise of their voices grew fainter, until, at last, all was still again.

While puzzling over these mysterious proceedings, I fell asleep, and slept undisturbed until the dawn of day, when I arose and anxiously looked about in order to discover the meaning of the strange noises and movements that had occurred in the night. Soon, little groups of natives approached me, with bland countenances ; but in answer to all my inquiries, they merely shrugged their shoulders and said, "Zambi te " ("Nothing at all ").

Determined to discover the matter, I took my fowling piece, and, on the pretense of going to shoot a guinea-fowl for my breakfast, I tracked the footsteps of the people who had rushed past my hut in such a state of excitement during the night. About two hundred yards off, in the scrub, as I walked along, I was suddenly horrified at the sight of a bloody head, and a few paces further on I saw the headless body of a naked woman. I subsequently found that the woman, together with others who had escaped to

WOMAN OF OUPOTO.

the forest in the darkness, had committed some trivial act of disobedience, for which she had thus been brutally murdered.

Above the Bangala and Mobeka tribes, we find the long line of Oupoto villages nestling at the foot of the green hills which here rise from the north shore of the Congo to a height of about two hundred to two hundred and fifty feet. The tribal brands are here quite different from those met with in any other parts of the Congo country; the entire face being one mass of cicatrization—circular lines of pimples larger than a pea rising from the skin around the eyes, over the forehead, down the cheek bones, and wherever a square inch of surface permits the hideous practice a free development.

CHAPTER VI.

THE Oupoto people are the nudest of the Congo tribes ; the
men are but lightly clothed with grass or palm-fiber cloth,
while the women go entirely naked, with no other covering
than that which the scarring and cutting of the skins of their
bodies afford them.

Cannibalism is as common in the Oupoto villages as it ever
was at Bangala ; slaves and prisoners of war being frequently
sacrificed to appease this unnatural appetite. Dogs are esteemed
greatly as a dainty dish, and are fattened up for food.

I had occasion once during my wanderings on the Upper
Congo, to approach one of these Oupoto settlements toward evening ; my party in canoes had the appearance of Arabs ; and, no
doubt, as we drew near, the natives took us for these marauders ;
for, on landing, we found the village empty. Every one had fled ;
the fires were burning brightly, and the pots containing the evening meal were left untouched on some of them, so hasty had been
the flight from the dreaded presence of the Arabs, whose evil
reputation had spread throughout their country.

We camped for the night in the deserted village, calling out at
intervals to the natives, who we concluded were hiding within ear-
shot, that we were their friends, and desired to purchase provisions
from them. During the night, no response came to our friendly

overtures ; but by early dawn, we were surprised over our morning meal by observing the figure of one of the savages emerging from the belt of forest at the back of the village plantations.

He crossed the manioc fields, and gained the plantain cover near the huts in which we had slept during the night, and from this point of vantage steadily regarded us and our surroundings. Satisfied with the result of his scrutiny, his keen eyes observing that we had damaged nothing, and had not pillaged his houses, he advanced to greet us. We were struck with his appearance, robust and vigorous, with the dignity of manner often observable in savages ; his scanty clothing revealing the muscular development of his frame. Around his neck he wore a necklace of human teeth and he carried by one of its hind legs a wretched dog of the breed of pariahs to be found in every Central African village. This unfortunate beast he held out temptingly to us, along with some pieces of uncooked flesh, spitted upon a stick, the nature of which we could only darkly conjecture, and in friendly tones he informed us that, as we appeared pretty well-behaved people from the respect we had paid to his goods and chattels, he concluded we were friends, as we assured him by our cries during the night, and here, as proofs of his good-will, he offered us the dog and the lumps of flesh to enable us to make a good meal, so as not to leave *his* village hungry.

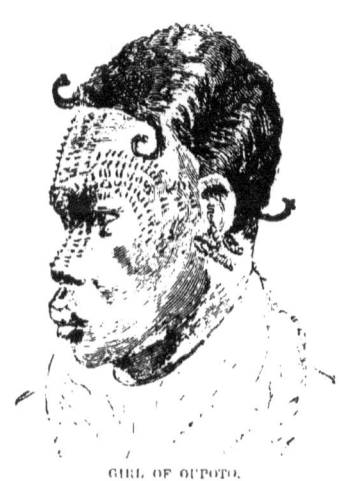

GIRL OF OUPOTO.

"AS PROOFS OF HIS GOOD WILL."

We could not even find words to thank our would-be host ; we declined both dog and human flesh (for such we discovered the other meat to be) with an emphasis that must have astonished our friend, and departed from his village horrified at the nature of the repast offered us, and yet feeling that the figure he cut upon the bank under his banana-tree, with the rejected dog yelping and howling in his arms, and a look of utter disappointment shadowing his features, was comical in the extreme, and one not often associated with acts of cannibalism.

AN ARUIMI TYPE.

Above Oupoto we find the fiercest savages of all the tribes yet discovered in the Congo Valley—those dwelling along the banks of the Aruimi River, from Basoko, at its mouth, up as far as it has been possible to ascend. What the earlier state of this country might have been, before the Arab invasion in search of ivory and slaves increased its confusion, it is impossible now to say, for the first white men to reach the Basoko found that the Arabs had already marauded through these territories, and had begun that system of attacking villages and carrying off their inhabitants to slavery, which we now find in full vigor along the course of the Aruimi, and as far to the north and east of it as our knowledge of the country extends.

AN ARUIMI SLAVE WOMAN AND BABY.

The result of all this is that each village is at strife with its neighbors. Every man fears all but the inhabitants of his own immediate vicinity; and should he be unfortunate enough to get caught by any of the neighboring tribes, he is killed and eaten, or perhaps sold to the Arabs, if his captors are on friendly terms with them. A state of the most complete disorder reigns through all the country, and it is a common thing to hear from the Arabs of the survivors from some village they have attacked being eaten by the neighboring villagers in whose lands they had fled for refuge.

On the other hand, this state of affairs is sometimes reversed, and the Arabs will themselves lose the day, and any of them falling into the hands of the natives are promptly killed and eaten.

which offense calls for fresh attacks on the "Wachongera meno" (tribes of the filed teeth), as they are termed by the Arabs, to revenge their losses. I was informed by Nassaro ben Sauf, an Arab leader, who had returned to the lower Aruimi from a raiding expedition far up that river, that the people there were armed with knives and bows and poisoned arrows, and that they had caught and eaten some of his people who were unfortunate enough to fall into their hands, and had even sent him their heads in the night, probably as a challenge, or to intimidate him.

On another occasion Selim bin Mohammed, the leader of Tippo Tib's detachment on the Aruimi, lost ten

A CANNIBAL SCENE WITH HUMAN FLESH ROASTING OVER THE FIRE.

men of his Manyema contingent during an attack upon the natives above the Yambuya rapids, directed by one of his lieutenants whom he had dispatched to that district.

Enraged at this loss, Selim determined the next day to ascend the river, with all his forces, and to exterminate the hostile natives. Upon reaching the scene of the conflict of the previous day, he found that the natives, to the number of two hundred, had escaped in canoes during the night, passing down stream, and that the few remaining in the village were endeavoring to get away in three canoes as he approached. He shot two of these and wounded several more. Landing, he found cooking-pots containing portions of the limbs and bones of the men killed in the first engagement, and their fingers tied in strings to the scrub on the river bank, where the natives had been forced to leave them when they ran the gauntlet down river.

During my stay on the Arnimi, I learned from the Arabs of the existence of a village of cannibals within a short distance of the spot where I was encamped. Accompanied by a Zanzibari lad named Majuta, who carried my bag, and by Fida, a native woman belonging to the Arabs, who was able to interpret the language of the natives into Kiswahili, Zanzibari tongue, I started one morning for this village. On arriving there, almost the first man I saw was carrying four large lumps of human flesh, with the skin still clinging to it, on a stick; and, through Fida, I found that they had killed a man this morning, and had divided the flesh. Subsequently I came across a party of men squatting round a fire, before which this ghastly flesh, exposed on spits, was cooking. Majuta, scared and horrified, rushed back into the bush, and I quickly quitted the village, satisfied with the truth of the stories the Arabs had related, and not desirous of witnessing any further confirmation of them.

Time and the influence of white men of upright character, as missionaries, traders and government officials, dwelling among them, and identifying their sympathies with the lives and welfare of the natives, will effect great changes in the people of the Upper Congo. As civilization spreads, and the ways of the white men become known to the dwellers in the far interior, a desire to imitate the more agreeable modes of living then presented to their gaze will spring up in the breasts of these poor African savages liberated by that time, let us hope, from the devastating scourge of Arab slave-raiding in their midst.

A CHIEF'S GRAVE.

CHAPTER VII.

Tippo Tib—Efforts to prohibit slavery by the powers—The Arab governor of
Stanley Falls—Livingstone's description of Tippo Tib—An amusing incident at Equator Station.

IN spite of efforts to prohibit the export of slaves from Zanzibar,
and in face of the opposition of more than one great European
power to their work, the Zanzibari Arabs of the East Coast
have penetrated into the most secret places of the middle zone of
the continent, and at the present day carry on their trade and ravage
the country, in defiance of the protests of civilization, and laugh
alike at the thunders of a blockading fleet or the commands of
their sovereign, the Sultan of Zanzibar.

The chief of these raiders, and at the same time, strange to
relate, the recognized representative of a government having for
its object the civilization of Africa and the rescue of its people from
these very raids, is Hamed ben Mohammed bin Juma, better known
as Tippo Tib.

He is both governor of the Congo Free State territory of Stanley
Falls, and leader of the Arabs who have established themselves in
that district, and whose object in coming there was one directly
opposed to the objects and policy of the Free State. It seems
strange, nay incredible, that the one man should represent two such
opposing sides, and yet, as I hope to make clear in this article,
Tippo can be a faithful enough servant of the government, while
still claiming the title of Arab leader, and exercising a powerful
influence over his compatriots—an influence which, although not

sufficient to check the indulgence of raiding instincts in his allies
and friends, is yet strong enough to preserve the peace of his own
immediate district intact, and cause those in want of slaves for
their caravans to the East Coast to go further afield in search of
victims.

In his dealings with the Congo Government, since his appoint-
ment to the governorship of Stanley Falls, Tippo Tib has striven as
far as possible to carry out the wishes of his European friends.
Wherever it lay in his power to help a white man, he has not been
chary of his assistance. Those travellers who have placed themselves in his power and demanded his aid, have no reason to com-
plain of the treatment they received from Tippo Tib.

Dr. Oscar Lenz and his companion, Baumann—the Swede
Gleerup—who crossed Africa, attached to Tippo's caravan, at the
time the Arab chief quitted the Falls previous to the outbreak of
hostilities between those he left in charge of his goods and the
officer of the State Station there—all experienced the kindness and
hospitality of one friend to another.

It is necessary to bear these facts in mind when criticising
Tippo Tib ; for it is possible for a good Mussulman (as Tippo
Tib claims to be) to be gentle, courteous and considerate of others,
when they come to him in the guise of friendship, and yet, at the
same time, to pour out the blood of infidels like water—nay more,
his religion commends the faithful son who helps to win over all
the world to the true faith, by exterminating unbelievers, and
there are surely none more unbelieving and heathen than the savages who come in contact with the Arabs in their marches through
Central Africa.

Therefore it is, that, while we find in Tippo Tib a gentleman of
bland Eastern politeness when dealing with white men (who,

although, alas ! unbelievers also, are still worthy of much respect) we see him at times ruthlessly cruel in asserting his authority over the savage tribes he finds it necessary to subjugate in his task of growing rich.

Now that that task is well-nigh achieved, Tippo is disposed, no doubt, to sit down contentedly on his heap of ivory and complacently survey his surroundings, while he makes friends of the white man.

In appearance, Hamed bin Mohammed is not unlike an old, white-bearded negro—for his skin is very black, due to the negro blood of his mother, and possibly of his grandmother, also—but there is an intelligence in his glance and a quickness of manner, which betray at once his descent from other ancestors.

Probably the descriptions contained in Livingstone's and Stanley's works, of their meetings with the even then renowned Arab, are the best pictures that could be presented of his appearance, save that years have brought with them their burden to bow the upright frame somewhat, and to scatter the snows of age over the once black beard.

Livingstone, in his "Last Journals," page 182, speaks of him as follows :

"July 29, 1869.—Went two and a half hours west to village of Ponda, where a head Arab, called by the natives 'Tipo Tipo,' lives ; his name is Hamid bin Mohammed bin Juma Borajib. He presented a goat, a piece of white calico, and four big bunches of beads, also a bag of holeus sorghum, and apologized because it was so little."

Again, on page 188, Livingstone says :

"The natives are quick to detect a peculiarity in a man, and to give him a name accordingly. The conquerors of a country try to forestall them by

TIPPO TIB.

selecting one for themselves. Susi states that when Tipo Tipo stood over the spoil taken from Nsama, he gathered it closer together, and said :

" 'Now I am Tipo Tipo,' that is, 'the gatherer together of wealth.' "

Stanley, coming later, in October, 1876, on his journey through the Dark Continent, gives a more vivid picture of his reception by Tippo, on page 95 of the second volume :

"Last came the famous Hamed bin Mohammed, *alias* Tippu Tib, or, as it is variously pronounced by the natives, Tipo Tib, or Tibbu Tib.

"He was a tall, black-bearded man, of negro complexion, in the prime of life, straight and quick in his movements, a picture of energy and strength. He had a fine, intelligent face, with a nervous twitching of the eyes, and gleaming white and perfectly formed teeth. He was attended by a large retinue of young Arabs, who looked up to him as chief, and a score of Wangwana and Wanyamwezi followers, whom he had led over thousands of miles through Africa.

"With the air of a well-bred Arab, and almost courtier-like in his manner, he welcomed me to Mwana Mamba's village, and his slaves being ready at hand with mat and bolster, we reclined *vis-à-vis*, while a buzz of admiration of his style was perceptible from the on-lookers.

"After regarding him for a few minutes, I came to the conclusion that this Arab was a remarkable man—the most remarkable man I had met among Arabs, Wa-Swahili, and half-castes in Africa.

"He was neat in his person : his clothes were of spotless white ; his fez cap brand new ; his waist was incircled by a rich dowlé ; his dagger was splendid with silver filagree work ; and his *tout ensemble* was that of an Arab gentleman in very comfortable circumstances."

It will be observed that Livingstone gives another translation of the nickname " Tippu Tib " than that I have generally heard as its explanation. On the Congo now it is accepted as having been bestowed upon him by the natives of the districts he first entered to wage war ; his many guns, with their quickly recurring discharges, sounding in the ears of the affrighted natives like " tip u tip, tip u tip," as the marauders blazed away through the plantations of their villages. Whatever the real meaning of the name, it is one that has clung to him, and it is now known far and wide through Central Africa, the tribes living near the Atlantic on the west having even caught up the magic syllables ; some Bakongo carrier, stumbling along with his heavy load in the Cataract region, will talk to his friend in the intervals of rest of the strange and almost visionary being who rules at far-off " Zingitini," and has as " many guns as the white man."

An amusing incident occurred at the Equator Station, when Stanley and his expedition halted there, on their way up to relieve Emin Pacha.

A native of the district came in to see the crowd of strange people who had disembarked from the flotilla of steamers, and were scattered over the grounds of the station, and going up to Tippo Tib, who was standing on the bank with Selim, his interpreter, he said :

"So you are going up to Zingitini ? I want to go there, too. I had a friend who fought with the white man (Deane) up there against Tippo Tib, and I want to go up to fight Tippo Tib."

CHAPTER VIII.

DURING my two or three sojourns at Stanley Falls, I came in contact with the leader of the Arabs on more than one occasion. He invited me to partake of his dinner or mid-day breakfast more than once, and these little *déjeuners sans fourchette* were among the most agreeable of my experiences during my stay in Africa.

The following story of Tippo Tib's life I gathered from the Arabs during my stay at Stanley Falls in 1889.

My chief informant was Selim bin Mohammed, an Arab factotum of Tippo's, and although I have reason to doubt the accuracy of all the incidents related by Selim, still, I think the story sufficiently reliable and interesting to give it almost as I heard it from my Arab informant.

Hamed ben Mohammed ben Juma is the grandson of Juma, and son of Mohammed ben Juma, both of whom were influential and wealthy merchants. The nickname, Tippo Tib, is generally used by the natives in speaking of him, but in the Kassongo and Nyangwe districts, he is commonly called by the natives Makangua Nzala, (*i. e.* afraid of hunger) the only thing, they say, he is afraid of.

He was born at Muscat, and is about fifty years of age. His

SELIM BIN MOHAMMED.

father was a half-caste
Arab, and his mother a
full-blooded negro slave
woman of Mrima. He
first entered the African
mainland with his father,
but on account of dis-
agreements, he split up
this connection, and ac-
companied his friend, Seid
ben Omar. He was at
that time, as he himself
expresses it, "a youth
without hair upon his
face." This partnership,
however, was also unsuc-
cessful, and he then com-
menced business on his
own account, and being
tolerably well off, was
able to gather together
one hundred fighting men
and equip them. With
four hundred natives
loaded with merchandise
he came into the interior,
trading cloth and beads
for ivory and slaves. He
reached the large village
of Ruemba, the chief of

which, a very savage, bad fellow, named Sama, was known to
Dr. Livingstone. Tippo Tib made a strongly fortified camp just
outside the fortifications of this village, the inhabitants of which
were the terror of the surrounding country, and were armed with
bows and arrows.

Many previous Arab traders who had visited Sama had been
murdered, and their goods stolen. At first no trade could be made,
and Tippo had almost decided to leave, but on the persuasions of
Sama, who said he had plenty of ivory, he stayed on, until he discovered a plot to murder him whilst he was engaged in trade, and
almost immediately after a disturbance broke out which Tippo Tib
regarded as an attempt to attack him, and so he replied with his
one hundred guns, shooting the natives down like sheep, through
the streets of their village. Sama himself was spared, as he
delivered over all his wealth, which consisted of more ivory than
Tippo could carry away, and he even had to burn most of his merchandise and all the smaller tusks.

After devastating the entire district of Ruemba, and forcing the
women and children into bondage, he discovered that a great friend
and countryman of his was not many days distant, but the road to
his camp was quite unknown. However, after a short interval,
he was visited by this fellow slave-trader, whose name was Seid
ben Ali, and who deplored the destruction of such an amount of
wealth, and at the same time upbraided Tippo Tib for his foolish-
ness.

"For," said he, "have you not subdued the whole district, and
could you not have taken a few hundred strong men as slaves to
have carried all your superfluous stock and the small ivory, and
put your one hundred guns in charge?"

Tippo Tib then made his way back to Zanzibar, realized on his captured ivory, and after about two years, during which time he gathered a large force around him, he again entered Africa, with the intention of making a " big haul." He was this time accompanied by a step-brother named Mohammed ben Masod, known by the natives as Kumba Kumba (*i. e.* one who gathers together) ; and on their way to Ruemba, the caravan was seized by an epidemic of sickness, and a very large number died.   This sickness occurred at a village named Gogo, between Zanzibar and Tabora.   Arriving at Ruemba, he met Dr. Livingstone, who was endeavoring to obtain porters to take him on to Ujiji and Tanganika.   Tippo Tib supplied his wants, and proceeded on his way to Tabora.   *En route*, he stayed to trade with a big chief named Rioua.   Here the natives were suffering much from hunger, as they had had bad crops, and, consequently, there were frequent disturbances between the natives and Tippo Tib's people ; various thefts having been committed by the natives, who were in the habit of lying in wait for Tippo Tib's women, when they engaged in collecting fire-wood, or in water-carrying, and stealing their loin clothes.   Tippo Tib had an audience with Rioua about the matter, but he could gain no satisfaction ; in fact, he was quietly ignored by the chief, who, interrupting the audience, got up to retire.   This aroused the quick temper of the Arab, who laid hands on him to detain him, whereupon the chief threw Tippo Tib on the ground.   There happened to be an armed man of Tippo Tib's suite near at hand, and he shot Rioua dead.   After this, there was war, and the natives fled.   Tippo Tib then decided to make a permanent camp at Ruemba, the former province of the vanquished Sama, and he left his step-brother Mohammed ben Masod in charge (he remained there until 1886); and he has retained the place until the present day.   At this period, Seid Madjid was Sultan of Zanzibar.

Tippo Tib then proceeded on to a large town called Rua, whose head chief was named Runga Kabari, and who was a particularly influential chief, gathering tribute from all the country round. Upon drawing near Katanga, the district of a minor chief named Msiri, they met a deputation from him, bearing eight large tusks of ivory, and a message that anything Tippo Tib required should at once be forthcoming, for the news of the defeat of the chiefs Sama and Rioua had spread over the country, and had intimidated the people. Seid ben Ali, who was accompanying Tippo Tib, decided to proceed on to the larger town of Rua ; so they parted, and some little time afterward, news was received that

Msiri had set upon Seid ben Ali, and had taken possession of everything he had.

Upon arriving at Rua, Tippo Tib formed a camp close to the residence of the king, but at first he found difficulty in entering into business transactions, as the entire population were well under the influence of their respective chieftains, who felt sore about the defeat of Sama and Rioua. Propositions were made that Kiombo, a minor chief, should act as middleman, and that the natives should bring their ivory to him, in order that he might negotiate with the Arabs, and in this way levy a kind of black-mail from Tippo Tib, and also from the natives themselves. But this arrangement did not meet Tippo Tib's views. He desired to send his men among the natives, and buy from them direct. This was refused, and things came to a standstill for some time, until, at last, there was a meeting arranged, and Runga Kabari, affect-ing great friendship, stated that he had sent for a supply of cattle, corn and other commodities, in order to present their visitors with a fitting present, and also, that he had decided to allow free trade with his people. This all appeared genuine, and Tippo Tib was on the eve of taking advantage of the permission to send his men about among the villages, when a native, to whom Tippo had taken a liking, and whom he had, from time to time, humored by small presents of beads and cloth, the like of which the poor fel-low had never seen before, came to him in the night, and stated that Runga Kabari and his chiefs had issued instructions to all his people to allow Tippo Tib's men to scatter as far as possible, and then to set upon them and destroy them, thus avenging the pun-ishments of Sama and Rioua. This was also verified later on by the old mother of the native, who told Tippo that the following day was to be the time of action, and that Runga Kabari's son-in-law, an exceedingly muscular fellow, had been deputed to act as Tippo Tib's assassin, and was to hang about accordingly the next day, to watch his opportunity.

The Arabs had, consequently, everything in readiness for a hard fight, and the following morning Tippo Tib, as usual, proceeded to the shed, which was erected near his camp for the purpose of receiving natives, and buying their ivory. Soon some natives came bearing some small tusks, and accompanied by the stalwart son-in-law, who inquired why Tippo Tib had not sent his men out.

A MANYEMA SOLDIER.

At this moment a commotion was heard outside, and Tippo Tib, in his eagerness, rushed out unarmed ; he was shot at with arrows by ambushed natives, and received two wounds, one in the thigh, and the other near the ankle. He was, however, closely followed by his two cousins, Shere ben Habib and Abdallah ben Habib, both of whom, being armed, avenged Tippo Tib's wounds with interest. Two of Tippo Tib's women, who were close by preparing food, rushed to his tent for his gun ; one received a fearful gash which nearly severed her head, the other, however, obtained the arms, and then Tippo Tib and his men routed the village, putting to flight the chiefs and people, and slaughtering many.

The chiefs thus routed sought refuge with other villages, but by this time Tippo Tib had gained such a name among them for prowess that they all feared to harbor the vanquished, and after conferring together, decided upon sending a deputation to seek peace with the successful Arabs. In the meantime, Tippo Tib's father, who was at a place called Kowendi, received false intelligence from the natives that his son had been defeated and all his people killed. He accordingly started off a re-inforcement to Tippo's assistance, but on their arrival at Rua, they were agreeably surprised to find how matters really were. Amid great rejoicings the deputation was received, and the terms of peace proposed were accepted, the Arabs allowing the chief to re-instate himself, on condition that he furnished men to act as guides, and pilot Tippo Tib and his people to countries where they could obtain ivory.

This was agreed to, and the caravan set out marching some distance to a large town named Kahoa, the chief of which was named Banzi Bondo. Here Tippo Tib halted, formed a camp, and

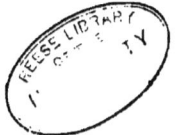

became great friends with Banzi Bondo's brother, with whom he entered into negotiations for the purchase of ivory, the terms being that the chief's brother should be intrusted with merchandise, and should proceed personally among the villages, purchasing on Tippo Tib's account, and that he should receive a percentage in goods, according to the extent of his purchases. This arrangement succeeded admirably, as the brother of Banzi Bondo was known as Tippo Tib's ally, and so fearful were the surrounding tribes that Tippo Tib should raid them, that they sought by presents and ivory to this brother to bribe him to keep his Arab friend at a distance.

Upon Banzi Bondo's return after his successful expedition, Tippo Tib was greatly pleased and surprised at the quantity of ivory he had obtained, and questioned him narrowly as to the district in which he had been purchasing. After some hesitation, he was informed that the most of the tusks came from Mbali, a place not far distant from Manyuema. Upon arriving here, he resorted to a clever stratagem which was attended with success. Whilst at Rua, he had learned from Runga Kabari that, many years before, there had been a war between Rua and Mbali, and that the king's two sisters had been taken as slaves, and had never since returned to their own country. These two women were the daughters of Muano Mapunga, and were consequently, as sisters of the aged king, persons of importance. All this information Tippo Tib had carefully noted, and upon reaching Mbali, he stated that he was the grandson of one of the sisters, and, consequently, nearly related to the king himself. This ruse succeeded in imposing on the people, the old king even abdicating in favor of Tippo Tib, **who he declared was the heir, as his sister's** grandson.

Thus Tippo Tib found himself suddenly the reigning sovereign of thirty or forty thousand people.

After a short time, during which he laid his plans, he started to conquer all the neighboring chieftains, thereby procuring much ivory.

At length he made up his mind to proceed on to Kassongo and Nyangwe, where there were other Arab merchants, and obtain news of the outside world and of how things went in Zanzibar, his six years of adventure having commenced to pall upon him. On his way he met with some opposition at a village named Isamba, but he speedily routed its inhabitants and proceeded on his way.

It so happened that a day or two after his departure from this place, some Arabs from Nyangwe arrived at the devastated village, and were informed by the natives that a large party of their countrymen, under Tippo Tib, had only just passed. These Arabs were, however, unacquainted with the name of Tippo Tib, but' knew him well by his proper name of Hamed ben Mohammed. In order to appear friendly to the natives, they told them they would hurry on after this Tippo Tib, and avenge the natives' wrongs ; but, in reality, they were very anxious to find out who the strangers really were. Great were the rejoicings when they overtook Tippo Tib's caravan, and discovered its leader to be their friend ; and altogether they travelled on to Nyangwe, where they found Commander Cameron, who had previously heard of Tippo Tib from Dr. Livingstone. Cameron, who was eager to obtain carriers and proceed on his journey, made arrangements with Tippo Tib.

There was some palaver, however, before this matter was settled, as Tippo Tib wanted badly to visit Kassongo before accompanying Cameron ; but the latter urged the matter, and explained the serious loss he was entailing by any delay, he having arranged to

complete his expedition in two years, and already one year had
passed.   Tippo Tib agreed to escort him and his gear to Rua, and
when they arrived there, Cameron joined some Portuguese traders,
and proceeded on his way to Banguela on the west coast.

Tippo Tib then retraced his steps, and reached Kassongo without any mishap.   Here he was at once elected, as being the most
influential and powerful of the Arabs, governor, over the heads of
the three former kings, Rusuna, Ngrue and Chupa, who paid
tribute in slaves and ivory.   (He still retains the supremacy, his
son Sefo being in command.)

CHAPTER IX.

Tippo Tib's capital at Kassongo—Meets Wissman at Tabora—An Arab defeat on the Aruimi—Tippo Tib revisits Zanzibar.

TIPPO TIB now made Kassongo his headquarters, and raided all the surrounding country. Stanley soon after arrived at Kassongo on his way "Through the Dark Continent," and arranged with Tippo Tib to accompany him down the Congo, a distance of several marches, and agreed to pay some five thousand dollars for the assistance. Tippo Tib agreed to accompany him sixty days. They came down, both by marching on the banks and in canoes as far as Vinga Njari, and Tippo Tib returned, collecting all his ivory and people together. Making his way over to Ujiji, at Ruanda, a powerful village six hours from Ujiji, which was occupied by a particularly wild tribe, who had guns, and who levied heavy dues upon travellers, and robbed without discrimination, he met with difficulties again from the natives. They attacked the rear of his caravan as it was passing through their village, captured some women, and also ivory and merchandise. Tippo Tib endeavored at first to obtain back the stolen goods and slaves quietly, as his guns now, owing to breakage and loss, numbered only eighty, and he was unwilling to fight with his weakened forces, fearing he should get the worst of it, with such a powerful tribe. However, they insolently refused to return anything, and challenged him to fight. Tippo Tib's reputation being thus at stake, he had to accept the challenge. He made a fierce attack and completely routed the villagers, gaining a considerable quantity of ivory, the people being wealthy, owing to their various robberies and the taxes they had for many years imposed upon passing caravans and neighboring tribes.

After being thus defeated, the people were anxious to make peace, and accordingly matters were settled. To this day the natives of that district are friendly, and have proved themselves useful in many ways to the Arabs.

Tippo and his large caravan then proceeded on until they came to Mrinza, which was governed by a king named Kassanora. This was also a powerful district, and the people had a few guns, and were very troublesome.

This king had a brother named Katarambura, who was ambitious and jealous of his brother, and when Tippo Tib arrived, he arranged with him to provoke a disturbance with the king, which should result in Tippo Tib's thrashing the villagers and enthroning Katarambura, who, on his part, agreed to pay a large quantity of ivory in addition to what Tippo Tib could himself obtain when sacking the villages.

Katarambura consequently entered into a series of petty disputes with the neighboring chieftains, and interfered in many ways with the king's authority. King Kassanora grew so angry at last that he sent a party of men to murder his rebellious brother, who, however, heard of the plot, and together with Tippo Tib, lay in wait for the king's men, who were on their way to carry out their instructions. The latter ran right into an ambush, and were cut in pieces. Tippo Tib then attacked the village, and it went hard with all but those who submitted. The king cleared out with a few of his followers, and sought refuge with Mirambo, the powerful king of Tabora, and at the same time endeavored to per-

suade Mirambo to make war with Tippo Tib, on his behalf This
Mirambo sternly refused to do, saying that Tippo Tib was his good
friend ; but he consented to act as mediator, with the result that
Tippo Tib allowed Kassanora to return to his country, but at the
same time enthroned Katarambura, who had fulfilled his promises
made before his accession to his brother's throne. The ex-king
Kassanora, then sought, by bribes to Tippo Tib, to secure his aid to
his own re-instatement. He made large presents of ivory, and
even gave his sisters to the Arab as wives. But Tippo Tib,
although he accepted these gifts, refused to take any further part
in the matter, consenting to neutrality only. Nothing was, however, done, and Tippo Tib, who had tolerably well drained this
country of ivory, pursued his way on to Ujiji with all his ivory
and slaves, and succeeded in making a permanent peace between
the Arabs settled at Ujiji under a man named Siki, and Mirambo,
the great king who had troubled Stanley when on his journey
across, and who had blocked the trade road for a considerable
time. This was a great stroke of business, and when, shortly
after, Tippo Tib arrived in Zanzibar, he met with a warm welcome
from the sultan, and also made a friend of Dr. Kirk, the British
consul.

When on his way down, he met the celebrated German traveler
Wissman at Tabora.

Tippo Tib remained one year in Zanzibar, and then again
entered Africa with a large caravan and many sheiks, and proceeded along the road which he had previously opened and made
known, to Stanley Falls, staying for short periods at Ujiji, Tabora,
and other places *en route*, where he had permanent stations under
responsible sheiks, for the reception and forwarding of his ivory
and goods, and also for keeping the road open.

Upon arriving at Stanley Falls, known to the Arabs as Zingiti, he decided to make his headquarters there; and about this time, Stanley, who had again returned to Central Africa, and was

engaged in founding the Congo Free State, placed a station there.

With Stanley Falls as a center, Tippo's men, in bands, under lawless Arab outcasts, made excursions to the various native villages

TIPPO TIB'S HEADQUARTERS AT STANLEY FALLS.

in the surrounding district, subjecting the people and catching slaves, which they bartered back to their own tribes for ivory.

Tippo Tib's men frequently met with defeat. For instance, a party under Selim bin Mohammed had found their way to the Arnimi River, after having been some time moving about devastating the country, and at a very populous village on the left bank, a few miles from the junction of the Arnimi River with the Congo River, named Basoko, they had formed a small, fortified camp; but one day, when the men were in the open village, the natives brought great quantities of palm wine, an intoxicating beverage, literally the fermented sap of the palm tree. The men were soon in a maudlin state of drunkenness. The Basokos, taking advantage of their opportunity, killed upward of seventy, cutting them to pieces with their big knives in a most horrible manner. Some took to the water; Selim, and a certain number—quite a few— escaped.

Tippo Tib again visited Zanzibar, accompanied by Dr. Lenz, in '86; and on his way, picked up Dr. Junker at Tabora.

CHAPTER X.

A MIDDAY HALT—GRANDEUR OF THE SCENERY—THE WHIRLPOOLS IN WHICH FRANK PO-
COCK WAS DROWNED—A TONIC SOUP FROM THE IRON WATERS OF NZUNGI—CAPTAIN
WALTER DEANE—OUR ENCAMPMENT.

IN November of 1886, I was journeying overland on my way
from Manyanga to Stanley Pool, in the Cataract region of
the Congo River, and on the second day's march, I halted
at midday near the native village of Nzungi, where a market was
being held on a hill-top. The site was remarkably picturesque.
Inland to the right, extended a rich country broken by deeply
wooded valleys and tree-covered hills, through the foliage of
which peeped the huts of numerous villages; while the pale-blue
columns of smoke from their fires floated away down the broaden
ing valleys to the great Congo, which thundered through a
gigantic chasm in the hills, about a mile away on the left. The
view to the north, reaching the elevated highlands on the opposite
bank of the Congo, was even finer. Two great streams, the Edwin
Arnold of Stanley's "Dark Continent" journey, and the Luculuzi
poured a white sheet of foam over a succession of steep precipices,
as they raced madly down from the hills to end their careers in a
headlong leap over the sombre cliffs which on that side rise sheer
eight hundred to one thousand feet above the hurrying waters of
the Congo.

Close to this grand scene, Frank Pocock, Stanley's aide on his
first journey across Africa, lost his life by the capsizing of a
canoe. After bearing all the terrible hardships of their great

journey, after seeing his brother die in the lake country, and after burying his other comrade, Frederick Barker, who also succumbed to the treacherous African climate, here it was, just upon the conclusion of that hazardous journey which had occupied nearly three years, that poor Frank Pocock was swept away in the mighty whirlpools of the Congo.

The level summits of these cliffs and many little overhanging patches of arable land which clung to their sloping sides as they rounded off inland, to again rise in other successions of steep terraces of rock, which at last mingled with the distant proportions of the rugged line of the Bwende hills, were covered with the palm trees and banana foliage of native plantations, and the eye could distinguish amid all the luxuriance of this vegetation the brown roofed houses of some tiny native village, crowning a jutting pinnacle of rock which leaned over the rapids and cataracts far below, or would follow, with a half-formed sense of wonder as to where it led, some native track winding away into the hills, showing for a moment clear and red as it traversed the iron-stone soil of the uplands, only to disappear in the sombre foliage which enveloped the next inland valley.

Beneath the shade of one of those graceful trees known as the "umbrella" tree, whose wide-spreading branches formed a cool resting place on the outskirts of the market, I stretched myself while waiting for the water to boil for my midday cup of tea, and I laughingly regarded the efforts of my so-called "cook" —a native youth from Manyanga—to make "beefsteaks" out of the limbs of a fowl, while he consigned the body, to which many of the feathers still clung, to the depths of a pot, whence it should later emerge, shriveled and shreddy, to figure as "boiled spring chicken" on my *menu*, while the liquid in which it had simmered, feathers and floating splashes of yellow grease all unskimmed, with a sweet potato or two bobbing about here and there through it, was dignified by the name of *potage aux poules,* or, as Maghasa, my *chef,* would have translated it, *moamba ma ususu.* Poor Maghasa! His endeavors that day to please me were all unavailing—for as my tea, which was first ready, very soon proved, the iron in the streams around Nzungi had entered into his soul—I mean into his cooking pots. The tea was a rich, slaty black, and tasted like tincture of steel; the soup would have made a capital tonic, and the sweet potatoes had such a coating of bluish black around them, that Maghasa's dusky cheeks paled in comparison as he offered me the pot containing this mess, while the fowl—but alas! poor creature, why enter into personalities? It had been strongly nurtured in its youth, no doubt, and had acquired a vast development of muscle and sinew in its struggles to escape just such a fate as this during every market-day around Nzungi for the last ten years, but now to its natural hardihood of frame were added the toughness and metallic hide the iron waters of Nzungi knew so well how to impart. I gave it to Maghasa with sincere pleasure, and my gratification was heightened by observing the contortions of his face, and listening to the clicking of his strong, white teeth, as they vainly endeavored to pierce those ribs of iron, or rend that frame of steel.

It was while engaged in this pleasing occupation, and while endeavoring to make a meal off the "beefsteaks," which, fortunately, had been fried without coming in contact with any of the mineral waters of the district, I heard a noise above the hubbub of the market, and saw the advancing leaders of a caravan pushing their way through the crowd of market people, as they came toward the tree under which I was squatting. They carried on their heads the effects of a white man—a tin trunk, a rifle, and a few of those odds and ends that figure on every African march— cooking utensils, an old chair, and a "chop box" (a box of European provisions).

In a few minutes, I could see, coming down the road from Stanley Pool, at a sort of jog-trot, a couple of natives, bearing a hammock, followed by others with the personal belongings of its occupant.

Starting up, I advanced to meet the white man I knew must be inside; and as the hammock men drew up in the throng of natives who crowded around, leaving their work of buying and selling, and ceasing their flow of talk for a few moments, to have a look at the new-comer, the awning of the hammock was lifted by a thin, wasted hand, and a pale, haggard face, with prominent cheek-bones and sunken eyes, was raised from the pillows to look at me; and I heard a voice saying :

"Hello, Ward, old man ! how are you ?" and the next moment I was grasping the hand of poor Walter Deane, the famous chief of Stanley Falls Station ; and, helping him to a place of shelter from the blaze of the midday sun, under the branches of the friendly umbrella tree, I could scarcely believe, as I looked at the wasted form, bent forward from weakness, the thin, tottering limbs and the feeble step, that this was the same Walter Deane whom I had seen but a few short months before, on his way up the Congo to take over the command of the outpost station of the Free State, then full of life and vigor, and confident of successfully accomplishing his difficult task—that of imposing restraint upon the lawless raiding of the Arabs, of inspiring the natives with a sense of security and confidence in the power of the Free State officials to protect them, and of winning over

Tippo Tib himself, the notorious chief of the Arab bandits, to regard the government established by Stanley, at that distant station of Stanley Falls, as entitled to his obedience and respect.

I arranged Deane as comfortably as might be on blankets and a rug under the tree, and while the natives hushed their noisy clamor, and either returned to the scene of their trading operations, or stood around with wide-open eyes, regarding the white man who had fought at far-off Kizingiti, and killed lots of the Arabs—for of all this the natives of the Bakongo country had heard from passing carriers—and they now learned from Deane's own men, some of them natives of that very district of Nzungi, that he was the identical white man.

I listened to the story from his own lips, of his gallant defense of the station against overwhelming odds, and of how he had finally been compelled to abandon his post, and of his thirty days' sufferings, without food or covering, in the woods, hunted day and night by the encircling bands of Arabs, until the arrival of Captain Coquilhat on his small steamer from Bangala, who extricated him and the survivors of his Houssa soldiers from their perilous position, and enabled him to return to Stanley Pool, whence he was now coming on his way back to Europe.

Deane's story was so interesting I can do no better than try and give it in his own words, as he told it to me in the Nzungi market-place.

CHAPTER XI.

"YOU know, Ward," said he, "how I was ordered to Stanley Falls last year by the colonel (Sir Francis de Winton, the administrator-general of the Congo State) to take over command, and to endeavor to keep the Arabs in order, and protect the natives from their exactions, so that the authority of the State might be established and fully recognized by them. Well ! you remember how I got wounded in the leg by a spear thrust when the Monungeri savages attacked us on the first journey up to the Falls, and how I had to return to Stanley Pool to recover from the effects of the wound, for we found that the spear had been poisoned. I lay ill a long while, and it was only in January that I was able to return again to the Falls."

I reminded him that all this was familiar to me, for I myself had accompanied him a portion of the journey up.

"Why, yes, of course, yes, I have been so ill, and have had so much medicine given me lately, that I fear my memory must be affected. Now, you remember, for I showed you my instructions, how I was promised a plentiful supply of ammunition and rifles and re-inforcements of men, when the river steamer *Le Stanley* made the next trip up to the Falls, which would be in August. Well, upon my arrival, I found things in a very bad condition, that the Arabs had the entire upper hand, and bullied

the natives just as they
pleased; yet I could do
nothing to prevent
them, for it was too far
off, the time of my ex-
pected re-inforcements,
to provoke any conflict
then.

" Tippo Tib had gone
back to Zanzibar and
had left his partner,
Bwana Nzige in charge
of his people, and
Nzige's son, Rachid bin
Mohammed bin Seid,
had also much to say in
the management of
affairs during Tippo
Tib's absence. I soon
saw that these fellows
did not like me or my
ways at all, and that I
shouldn't get them to
conform to my orders
without a row. I
had thirty-two Houssas
under Sergeant-Major
Musa Kanu, a fine, tall
fellow—you know him
—and also about forty

RACHID BIN MOHAMMED.

Bangalas whom I had brought up with me on *Le Stanley,* and I
set to work to fortify the station, clear away the grass and scrub
around it, in case of a surprise, and to be able to keep my eyes on
the Arabs over on the mainland."

It is necessary to observe that the State Station of Stanley
Falls was built on an island in the Congo just below the seventh
cataract, while the Arabs were mostly on the mainland, although
a few lived in a village on the same island among the natives.

"Well, the time went on, and a worse feeling sprang up between the Arabs and myself, owing to my attempts to protect the
natives from their robberies. One day, about the middle of July
(1886), a woman entered the camp seeking protection and saying
that the Arabs had flogged her. Her story was that she was the
daughter of a big chief away up in Kassongo and that she
had been given to Tippo Tib as a pledge of friendship by her father,
but that being of the Wachongera meno tribe (*i. e.,* of the 'filed
teeth' tribes who are usually cannibals) Tippo Tib did not care for
her, and had given her to one of his most influential Arab headmen. This Arab ill-treated her, she said, and so she fled to us for
refuge. I could not discover any traces of ill-treatment; there
were no marks upon her skin; and I told her that she must return
to her Arab husband as I had no right to interfere unless she were
being cruelly used; and I had her conducted back to the Arab
village. After a few days, she came into the station again, with
her back cut with lashes from a whip, and her body covered with
bruises, telling us that she had been terribly flogged, and that,
had she not escaped, her master would have killed her. This time
there was no doubt her story was true. She was a pitiable-look-
ing object, and I determined nothing should induce me to give her
up again to the cruelty and brutality of the Arabs. It was not

STREET IN NATIVE VILLAGE AT STANLEY FALLS.

long before Bwana Nzige, with his son Rachid, and all the principal Arabs, came over to me and demanded the woman's release.
I replied that I should not think of letting her be taken away
again to suffer their
brutal violence, and that
I was sent to the country
to prevent such acts as
this, and that, as the
representative of the
Congo Free State, I in-
tended to do my duty.
As the woman repre-
sented a certain value to
them, I was quite pre-
pared to pay, on behalf
of the government,
whatever they should
demand, in reason, as
her ransom. They sul-
lenly declined this offer,
and persistently de-

"SAPENA," THE DAUGHTER OF THE KASSONGO CHIEF.

manded the release of the woman, saying that I should
regret my refusal. Then I knew that the storm which had
been so long brewing was going to break. However, we were
well armed; my Houssas were plucky, and the fortifications I
had constructed protected us well, and I considered that with the
aid of my two Krupp guns we could keep the Arabs at a respectful distance, and in a few days, for it was the month of August, I
hoped to see *Le Stanley* arrive with re-inforcements and ammunition, and a white officer or two, for I was alone as you know. The

Arabs made no direct attack upon us, although large numbers of their Manyemas continued to assemble on the mainland. At last, *Le Stanley* was signaled, early one morning, coming up the river, and I was indeed delighted, for I expected she would have on board the much needed ammunition and re-inforcements. But imagine my disgust, Ward, when, on getting to the landing-place, I found she had not brought me a single cartridge of the promised ten thousand—not a rifle, and not a man, save only Lieutenant Dubois, of the Belgian Lancers. He turned out to be a splendid fellow ; but still I needed the other things, or my fight was hopeless."

Here Deane broke off his story, for the exertion of talking so much had exhausted him.

By this time, our tents had been pitched on a grassy plain close by, as we had decided to camp together for the night ; and after sundown, when our men had gathered around their camp-fires, and were busily engaged eating baked yams and story-telling, Deane brightened up again, and, as he lay upon a native mat, propped up with blankets and light baggage, in front of our own cheery log fire, he resumed his story, speaking so quietly and deliberately that one would almost have been under the impression that he was relating some romance, instead of the story of his own heroic defense of his station against the Arabs.

" Well, when *Le Stanley* arrived, the Arabs came to the conclusion that I should prove too strong for them with my supposed re-inforcements ; so they sent in a deputation to intimate that hostilities were at an end, and that they desired to remain in friendly relations with the white man who represented the Congo Free State. I agreed to this, and we parted seemingly good friends, and shortly afterward, I even went so far as to visit one of their villages at the upper end of the island, and there I found,

IN FRONT OF OUR OWN CHEERY LOG FIRE

to my chagrin, some of the Zanzibari crew of *Le Stanley* chatting with their compatriots among the Arabs, and telling them of my disappointment, and how the steamer had brought me none of the expected aid.

" The next day, *Le Stanley* left, and Dubois was busy arranging

LE STANLEY.

his quarters, while I glanced through the piles of newspapers that my considerate friends on the Lower Congo had sent up to me. Toward evening, I was told by a friendly native that the Arabs intended attacking the station the following morning, for he had overheard their plans. We kept strict watch during the night, but could distinguish nothing, until at dawn we found, sure enough, a large party of Manyemas had crossed from the mainland in the night, and had intrenched themselves on my island, about eight hundred yards from the stockade. As soon as it was light, we received a practical proof of their hostility, for they fired upon

A LEADER OF MANYEMA MARAUDERS.

us. We kept up a lively fire upon them for two days with our Snyder and Martini rifles, but they were well sheltered by their rough earthworks, and there were no serious losses on either side.

" Our men kept up a tremendous fusilade whenever the Arabs made any signs of attacking, and, on the evening of the third day, Dubois sallied out of the stockades and penetrated into the Arab lines, capturing a Manyema drum which they left in their flight. It was hot work, and he got his revolver pouch shot off his hip. That night they remained quiet, but in the morning fresh earth heaps were found thrown up nearer our intrenchments, and the fight recommenced. Our ammunition was now beginning to fail, and so we could not waste so many shots, and the Arabs took advantage of this to make two or three rushes right up to our position; but we drove them back each time, and I worked the Krupps so hard that blood came from my ears, and I knocked the end off my little finger by getting it jammed in the breech. My boys, Jack, poor little Jack from Manyanga, down there in the valley, and the two Aruimi youngsters behaved splendidly, bringing ammunition to us and making tea and carrying the cups up to us right across the Arab line of fire. Dubois charged out again and drove them back, and then darkness set in and stopped the fight for the night. The Bangalas deserted that night, taking some native canoes, and making off down river to try and reach Bangala, which you know is a five hundred miles' journey.

A MANYEMA WOMAN

"In the morning the fight started again. We could now do little but work the Krupps, as the little rifle ammunition we had left was almost entirely bad. We got cap guns and old trade flint-locks out of the store and gave them to the Houssas to fire; but seven of these poor chaps were already dead, and the rest, all save Musa Kanu and three men, came to me in the evening and said they must go; that it was no use fighting when they were bound to fall into the hands of the Arabs. I threatened to shoot them as deserters, and they replied:

"'Very well, master, you shoot us; we would rather you shoot us than have our throats cut by the Arabs.'

"And as soon as darkness set in, they made off to the canoes and drifted down river after the Bangalas.

"Dubois and I were now left with only four Houssas and Samba, a native of the Aruimi, who had been freed by the State, and worked faithfully with me during all my stay at the Falls, and despairingly we determined to destroy that night all that we could of the stores remaining, to spike the guns, and blow up the station, and make off to the woods, to hide until relief should come from Bangala, where we reckoned the fugitive Bangalas would arrive by a certain date, and Coquilhat would hurry up in the steamer *A. I. A.* (*Association Internationale Africaine*) to our relief. We sprinkled the stores with oil, piled up the cartridges, spiked the Krupps, and gathered all the loose gunpowder together; and having set a train to this outside the station, we two, with Musa Kanu and his three faithful Houssas, and Samba, who refused to budge without us, made off under cover of the darkness, to gain the north shore and seek shelter in the woods there.

"I was the last to leave the place, and I set fire to the train of powder and made after the rest."

CHAPTER XII.

"THE night was pitch dark and the station was blazing behind us, but somehow the gunpowder had not exploded. We knew the Arabs must have discovered our flight by this time, so we hurried along to cross over to the mainland. We had to wade through an arm of the Congo, a rushing torrent of water about fifty yards wide, and generally at that season only waist deep. Dubois slipped on the rocks and was swept down into deeper water. I knew he could not swim, so I at once jumped in after him, and managed to catch hold of him before he was carried away by the swift current. We were just able to reach the steep, rocky bank, and exhausted, I told Dubois to hold on to the edge of a jutting rock, while the Houssas, having safely passed over, came to our assistance along the top of the bank. Musa Kanu undid his belt and gun-strap, tied them together and lowered them to me, but when I turned to where Dubois had been, saying, "Catch hold here," I could see nothing of him ; there was no Dubois. By the light of the burning station, where the cartridges and gunpowder had now commenced to explode, illuminating vividly for the moment the surrounding scene, I searched the waters for any sign of poor Dubois, but alas, poor fellow, he had become numbed in the water, or his heavy boots pulled him down, and he had been swept away by the current. It was the last I ever saw of him, and my grief and misery were so great at the loss of my only friend away up there, after all the pluck he had shown during the four days' fighting at the station, that I wept, while the Houssas, after pulling me up, cried too.

"We were, indeed, a wretched lot. My clothes had been burnt off me and torn in the fight. I had only an old blanket around me and a shirt on, and no boots; and sadly, and feeling that I didn't care if the Arabs should find me and end the wretchedness at once, I crept away into the forest.

"For thirty days we remained in hiding there. Often we could hear the Arab gang beating the woods around our retreats, for every night we changed our quarters. The natives, who were friendly all through the business, came often to tell me where the Arabs were looking for us, and to bring me little offerings of manioc and plantains. We lived on what we could pick up in the forest—green leaves, roots, and caterpillars frequently—or on the scanty stock of food the poor natives were able to convey to us in secret; for they feared being watched, and that our hiding-places should become known to the Arabs.

"At last, on the thirtieth night, they came to me and said that our retreat had been discovered, and that I must fly, but I was too weak to stand even then. I could only crawl, and I knew Coquilhat would be up on that very day; for thirty days was the time I reckoned it would take him to come up, on hearing of our defeat from the Bangalas who had bolted. I was carried down at night into a canoe the natives brought, and we drifted off down the stream. I told the men to keep a good lookout for the steamer, for I felt certain she would arrive that day. However, we saw nothing. The poor Houssas slept, and, at early morning, we were alongside a village on the right bank. It was no use going any

"MUSA KANU UNDID HIS BELT AND GUN STRAP."

further; we should miss the steamer among the islands, and fall
into the hands of the Arabs, who were looking out everywhere
along the shore for us. So we landed here, and I crawled up the
bank toward the village. The natives saw us and came rushing
out. One fellow ran at me with his spear raised to hurl. I looked
up at him and pointed my revolver, which had never left me; he
lowered his arm, and then took another step forward, and poised
his spear again, steadily regarding me all the while. Suddenly he
yelled: '*Mzungu, mzungu!*' (the white man, the white man), and
throwing down his spear, rushed up the bank toward the others,
crying out that we were the white man's party from Kizingiti.
They carried me up to their houses, gathered round us with cries
of delight, and brought food and all the best things of their villages.
Then they told us how they had looked for us ever since the loss
of the station, and that, best news of all, the steamer had passed
up yesterday toward the Falls with two white men, asking for
news of us everywhere; and the canoes coming down reported
that fighting was going on between the Arabs and the steamer.
I knew now our troubles were nearly over. The natives sent off
men to tell Coquilhat that I was found, and Samba went to a
point from which he could survey the river through the trees
unobserved. Soon we heard a cry from Samba : '*Mashua, mashua
ana kuja!*' (the steamer, the steamer is coming); and Coquilhat,
hearing Samba's cries from the bushes, put into the bank, picked
up poor, naked old Samba, and in a few minutes had steamed up
to our hiding-place, and I was on board the *A. I. A.* safe and sound
—well, as sound as I could be after my thirty days' starvation in
the forest.

" We got down to Bangala all right, where I found some of the
fugitive natives and my Houssas. Others of them had been captured and eaten by the Oupoto cannibals.

Q

" From Bangala I was brought down to Leopoldville, and after getting somewhat stronger and able to endure the journey down country, here I am, on my way home; and I hope soon, Ward, old chap, to be as right as ever, and able to come back for another fight with the Arabs. If the governor will give me two hundred men, I'll go up again now, weak as I am, and retake the station and drive the Arabs back to Nyangwe !"

Thus it was that poor Deane told me during our long chat together at Nzungi, how the Falls station had been lost, and how, where the blue flag with the golden star, the emblem of the Free State, had formerly floated, now waved the red ensign of Zanzibar, over the stronghold of the slavers. It was sad news; and the death of poor Dubois was the worst of all, for he was a man but newly come to the Congo, and one every body liked.

This was the last I saw of poor Deane, whose caravan started at the first gray dawn of the following morning. I watched the long line of native carriers wending their way along the serpentine path which led toward the coast. Every now and then they disappeared over the brow of a hill, only to re-appear a few minutes later on some further summit, where I could see the flutter of the white awning over Deane's hammock, as the bearers hurried it along in the cool morning air. After a few months in Europe, Deane returned to the Congo to shoot elephants, and met an untimely death in the forests of Lukolela from a wounded elephant.

No attempt was made by the government of the Congo Free State to retake the Falls, and the Arabs were left in undisputed possession of all the territory above Oupoto, where they extended their ravages unchecked, and became the virtual, if not the lawful, masters of the land.

Such was the state of affairs at Stanley Falls, and in that part of Central Africa, when H. M. Stanley arrived at Zanzibar *en route* for the Congo, to engage men for his long journey up that river and across to Wadelai, on the Nile, to bring rescue or relief to Emin Pacha.

One of the first to greet Stanley at Zanzibar was Tippo Tib. Years had elapsed since they met before in the wilds of Africa. Tippo had since then augmented his power. His name was now known from Zanzibar on the east far to the west of Tanjanyika, to the headwaters of the southern affluents of the Congo, and down that river to the Free State station of Bangala, which now alone remained between the Arabs and Stanley Pool. They had parted friends, Stanley and Tippo, and it was the policy of neither now to rake up the old animosities of their respective sides. Tippo was anxious for the friendship of Stanley, and for his great influence to be used with the authorities of the Free State to secure recognition of his position as master in the Stanley Falls district, and that an outlet might be opened down the Congo to the Atlantic for his ivory, saving him the expense and fatigue of the long overland journey to Zanzibar.

Stanley, on his side, wished to see the authority of the State re-imposed at the station he had himself founded years before, and he also desired that friendly relations might be established between white men and Arabs on the Upper Congo, so that, with the advancing influences of commerce and civilization, the slaver might recognize that legitimate trade in ivory and the produce of the interior could bring with it rewards as great as those he now derived from his infamous traffic in human beings.

It might have been possible for the State to have recovered Stanley Falls by fighting, and to have driven the Arabs back, but that would have resulted in effecting only one of Stanley's objects. The Arabs would then have been hopelessly hostile, and for years to come Central Africa would have resounded, through all its forest swamps, with the din of murderous conflict and the cries of poor creatures still being dragged away into slavery. When, therefore, Tippo Tib presented himself before him at Zanzibar, Stanley received him kindly. Tippo's entrance had been a dramatic one, it is said; for, turning to his attendants, he bade them uncover a Krupp shell they carried, and, showing it to Stanley, said :

" This is what your people gave me as presents at Zingiti (Stanley Falls) after you left. This is how they showed the friendship of the white man for the Arab."

When the fight with Deane broke out at the Falls, Bwana Nzige had dispatched one of the shells fired from the fort, to Zanzibar, with a message to Tippo Tib that this was what they were getting from the new white man ; and Tippo now came forward as the injured individual to tell his tale of wrongs to Stanley, and to smooth matters over by representing his side as having most unwillingly engaged in the conflict with the Free State.

Letting by-gones be by-gones, Stanley accepted the excuses of the Arab chief, and telegraphing home to King Leopold II. of Belgium, received his assent to the scheme proposed, which was nothing less than to enlist Tippo Tib on the side of the government, and to make him State Governor of Stanley Falls District. This was, indeed, of course, taking the bull by the horns, to place in a position of highest trust and authority the man who, although absent from the scene, was primarily responsible for the destruction of Stanley Falls Station ; but it was, without doubt, the only peaceable solution of the question, and the sole method of reimposing the Free State authority in those regions without bloodshed and an expenditure of money the government of the little State was not at that time in a position to incur.

The following reply of Stanley at the Cape, *en route* for the Congo with Tippo Tib, on board the steamer *Madura* with him, to a remark about his trusting such a renowned bloodthirsty slaver, reveals the light in which he regarded the transaction. With his usual calm, immovable expression of countenance, he answered that—

" 'There is more joy in heaven over one sinner that repenteth than over ninety and nine just persons who need no repentance.' "

That Tippo, too, felt the responsibilities of his new post may be gathered from the tone of his reply to a missionary at Banza Manteka, on the Lower Congo, where the relief column marching to Stanley Pool halted for a night.

Tippo bore the reproach of the missionary with much grace, that he had indulged in awful massacres, and how terrible would be the number of lives he must account for at last; and then, with his customary benevolent expression, he replied :

"Ah, yes ! I was a young man then ; now you see my hair is turning gray ; I am an old man and shall have more consideration."

In the summer of 1887, Tippo arrived at Stanley Falls, and was formally installed in his new post as governor of the district in the name of the sovereign of the Free State— King Leopold II. and the blue flag with the gold star once again waved over the lone station in mid Africa. Since its destruction in the fight against Deane, the Arabs had neglected the buildings of the station, and Tippo now chose as his residence the village on the south mainland overlooking the island on which the fight had been waged.

To enable himself to keep informed with the necessities of his

post, and in touch with the authorities of the Free State at Boma,
Tippo requested that a white officer might be sent to him to act as
his secretary and to translate to him the letters he might receive
from the governor-general, or put into official language his own
sentiments on the state of the district intrusted to his charge.

This request was complied with, and a young Belgian lieutenant
was dispatched to Stanley Falls, where for several months he
remained practically the guest of Tippo, accompanying him on his
journeys, and advising him as far as possible.   Tippo's position,
however, was no easy one, for the government of the Free State
at Boma was never satisfied with the sincerity of his professions
of friendship ; and the anomaly of being represented among the
savages of the Falls by the man who was acknowledged as the
head of all the slave gangs which had ravaged that very country
for years, was one the government did not relish, and they sought
the first occasion of dispatching (quite in a friendly way, of course)
a Belgian officer, accompanied by a white assistant, with an
exceedingly small force of armed men, to re-occupy the abandoned
station on the island, and assume its control, acting in the name
of the government as *Commissaire de District.*

This was a slap in the face to Tippo, who held his commission
from Stanley as governor of the entire country, from the mouth
of the Aruimi up to Nyangwe ; but, affecting not to observe the
slight cast upon his expressions of fidelity, the wise old Arab
received the new-comers affably enough ; welcomed them to *his*
territory, and expressed his pleasure that they should be going to
live so near one another, where, no doubt, they should be good
friends.   At the same time Tippo notified the Chief of Bangala
Station, some hundred miles lower down the Congo, and which
was the next government post to his, that he regarded the Aruimi

MARKET SCENE AT STANLEY FALLS.

River as the boundary of their respective districts. Below that point the Chief of Bangala might act as he pleased ; above it, all the country was within the jurisdiction of the Falls.

While Tippo was thus acting the part of governor of a huge territory, his subordinates and allies—Arabs from Muscat and negroes from Zanzibar—were establishing themselves throughout the land, not only within the points ruled by Tippo, but far beyond those limits, and were appearing at many points in the Congo State where the presence of Arabs had never before been suspected. Down the Itimbiri River, which falls into the Congo from the north, between Bangala and the Aruimi, bands of ivory and slave-hunters appeared. On the upper waters of the Malinga, which enters the Congo *below* Bangala, they were even reported by the natives as having formed encampments ; and far down to the south and west, the Sankuru tributary of the Kasai was overrun with their canoes.

Rachid bin Mohammed ben Seid Marajib (Rachid the son of Mohammed, the son of Seid of Marajib, a district in Muscat where he was born) had occupied the mouth of the Lomami River, that great tributary which drains so large an extent of country and empties into the Congo opposite the Aruimi ; and all up its course the Arabs had penetrated.

Wherever the eye turned on the map of Central Africa, in the regions bordering on the Congo, might be traced the line of Arab advance, and the different trading steamers, which sought the many affluents in search of ivory, all returned to Stanley Pool in the year 1888 with the same stories, that on the upper waters of nearly every tributary above the equator, as well as on those of the Kasai and Oubangi, there were indications and stories of Arab encroachment.

This was the position which faced the Free State government, and to avoid the possibility of any recurrence of the Stanley Falls fight in Deane's time, or a like event happening perhaps at Ban-

STANLEY FALLS.

gala should the Arabs be permitted to continue their advance. it was determined to form three fortified camps, of five hundred men each, on the Aruimi, Lomami and Sankuru rivers.

The first of these was established in December of '88. and although friendly relations are still continued between the officers in charge of the camp and Tippo Tib. it only requires a very little friction to lead to another outbreak of hostilities.

That Tippo himself desires peace, and to abide faithfully by his contract with Stanley, I fully believe ; but then, there are many other Arabs, and many of their followers, who are not actuated by such motives. They desire to make fortunes, to get as much ivory and to gather as many slaves, to occupy as fertile and pleasant a country as it is possible to find ; and it is in their search for these commodities and this happy resting place, they will come into

contact with the armed forces of the Free State, and provoke a
conflict that may mean the extinction of the effort to civilize
Central Africa, if the young Congo government is left alone to
battle with its barbarous foes ; or, on the other hand, that may
mean the destruction of that organized system of terrorizing,
slave-raiding and robbery which now holds undisputed sway over
the region aptly called the " Heart of Africa."

PART III.

CANOE JOURNEY.

CHAPTER I.

FIFTEEN HUNDRED miles from the nearest sea-shore, and
situated almost upon the Equator, is the famous Arab settlement of Stanley Falls, known to the Arabs and native inhabitants as "Kizingiti," meaning "barrier," in reference to the cataract which effectually bars all progress by river past this point.
This barrier was the last obstacle encountered by Stanley in the

navigation of the river, on his memorable journey through the Dark Continent, ere he swept into the tranquil expanse of broad waters which extends from these falls, uninterrupted by rapid or cataract, to Stanley Pool, a distance of eleven hundred miles.

Hamad bin Mohammed, familiarly known to the world as "Tippo Tib," the Bismarck of Central Africa, resides here, and has accumulated a vast amount of ivory by plundering the neighboring savages who reside in the unexplored forest regions, where countless herds of elephants also make their homes, roaming alike through the dismal swamps hidden in the heart of the forest, and the rich banana and plantain gardens of the native villages.

Sixty miles below Stanley Falls, in the midst of a populous native village, on the south bank of the Congo, at the confluence of the Lomami River, a young Arab, named Rachid bin Mohammed, the son of Nzige, Tippo Tib's confidential adviser and partner, had built a roughly fortified camp; and it was from here, on April 3d, 1888, that I started on my first long canoe journey down the Congo, to carry dispatches to the coast, and to communicate to Europe news of vital importance to the work on which I was engaged.

Procuring two large native war canoes, which had been hewn

out of solid trees, I lashed them side by side with vines, tying
batons of wood across the gunwales to steady them.   After caulk-
ing up the leaks, fitting dunnage wood along the bottom, and
rigging up a rough frame with sticks, over which I fastened my
old, patched tent, to form a shelter from the fierce tropical sun
and the heavy night dews, and stowing away my scanty baggage
and ammunition, I was ready for a start.

My crew consisted of thirty Wangwanas, men of Zanzibar, a
reckless, happy-go lucky set, who had all been so accustomed to
roughing it since childhood, on long, weary caravan journeys
with the Arabs, that the novelty of danger had long since worn
off.   I had with me, also, five Soudanese soldiers from the ranks
of the Egyptian forces at Cairo.   These men were of a warlike
disposition, and particularly partial to a meat diet.

Although willing and bright, yet none of my men were accustomed to canoe paddling, so that our progress depended more on
drifting with the current than upon our own individual efforts.

I had before me a journey of several hundred miles through a
thickly populated country of more or less hostile savages, whose
cannibal assaults upon Stanley's heroic band, on the occasion of
his first descent of the Congo in his flotilla of canoes, boded ill to
any who might venture upon the same journey in like craft.   Our
greatest danger lay in the fact that for the first two hundred
miles the natives had been continually harassed by Arab marauding expeditions from Stanley Falls ; and owing to the character of
my crew, and the resemblance their costumes bore to those of the
slavers, it was highly probable we should be mistaken for a band
of the same gentry, and greeted with the welcome they were
accustomed to accord such visitors.

Rachid bin Mohammed, whose long experience as a marauding

leader eminently qualified him to express an opinion upon the subject, shook his head and said:

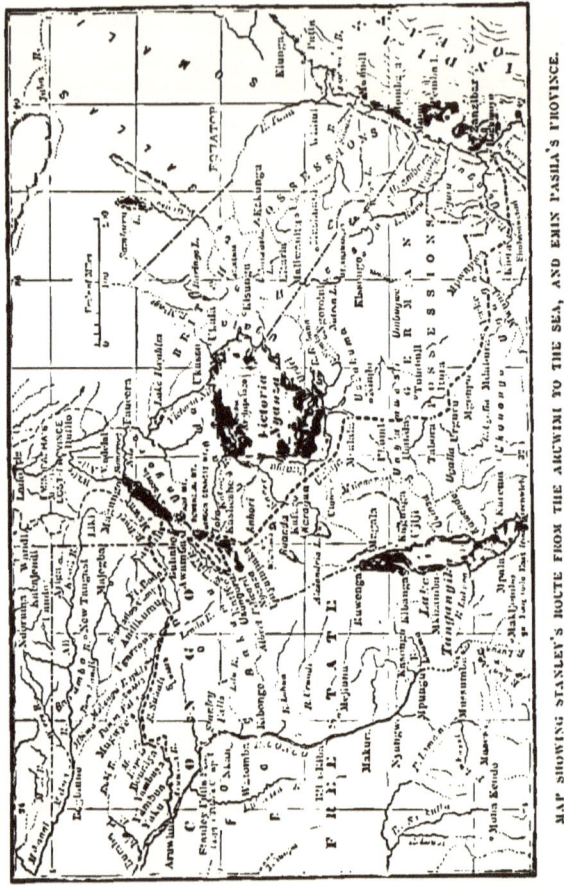

" You will never pass the savages at the mouth of the Arnimi River in those two canoes, with so few men. It is impossible:

you will all be killed and eaten by the Wachongera meno (tribes of the filed teeth). Think again before you throw away your life."

The duty before me was imperative, and Rachid's warning passed unheeded. Still it was not pleasant to find such an old campaigner taking such a serious view of the undertaking. My own men I could plainly see looked on the venture as a desperate one, and it was only by dint of cheery speeches and a confident demeanor that I could arouse them from despondency and encourage them to exertion. It was just past noon as we pushed off our unwieldy craft, amid the deafening shouts of farewell from the multitudes of Arab followers and natives who crowded along the muddy bank of the river to see the last of us.

" Kwa heri, Kwa heri, bwana," (good-bye, good bye) echoed after us as we drifted out into the stream.

Before starting we had, of course, laid in a good stock of provisions, for we could not expect to purchase anything from the natives dwelling within the sphere of Arab persecution. Our live stock consisted of several fowls, with their legs tied together to prevent them from flying away, and two goats, which lay on a bunch of grass, philosophically chewing their cud. We had enormous bunches of green bananas and plantains, sweet potatoes, and an abundance of sour-smelling cassava root, which, when soaked, pounded, rolled in banana leaves and boiled, forms the staple food of most Central African tribes.

Our guns were lightly lashed to the gunwale next to each man's seat, and I issued a few rounds of ammunition for use in case of any sudden attack. During the afternoon, we drifted lazily along with the current, while the men were busy stowing the provisions and settling themselves in comfortable positions to paddle.

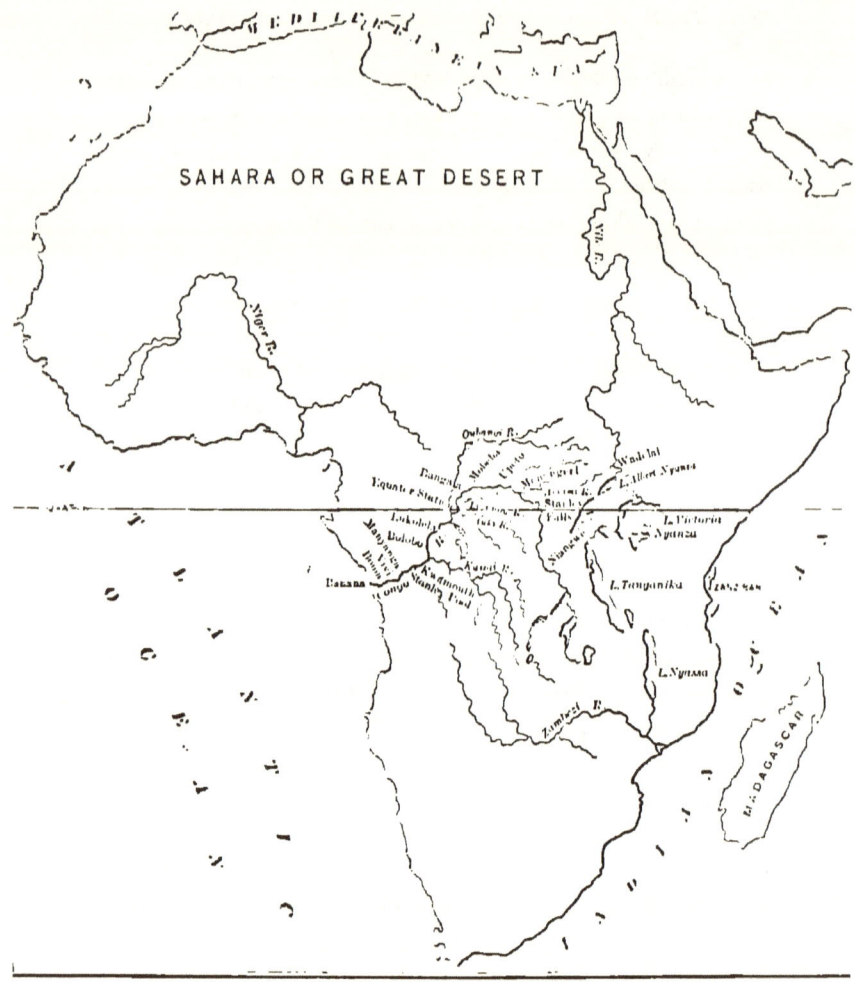

MAP SHOWING THE COURSE OF THE CONGO.

We went along better than I expected, and by about 5 P. M.
were in sight of the low forest islands opposite the populous
villages of the savage Basoko tribes at the mouth of the Aruimi
River.

War drums resounded on both sides of the river, and as it grew
dark, we could distinguish large canoes, containing armed natives,
following us in the distance. By midnight, in the dim starlight,
we discerned a dark mass of canoes drawn up across the river.
They were hostile natives, lying in wait to attack us ; and we all
prepared for war ; but fortunately, as we approached, they opened
out and allowed us to pass, yelling and threatening us from the
shelter of a neighboring island. The word "Niama," meaning
" meat," was frequently distinguishable, and sounded ominously
to our ears, for these people are voracious cannibals, and our fate
was obvious should we fall into their hands. The ease with
which we had avoided the first serious difficulty in our way
seemed to infuse fresh spirit into my men. They, like all their
kind, were fatalists, and if we had suffered mishap at this early
stage of the journey, they would have had no heart to meet the
trials and perils that lay before them. I noticed a change at once
in their bearing and aspect, and instead of whispered murmurs of
discontent, I could hear the paddlers humming the refrain of
some old chant of triumph as they pushed the canoes through the
water.

A little later we sighted another large dark mass in the middle
of the river, and steered for it, under the impression that it was a
group of hostile canoes, preferring to be the attacking party to
waiting until a larger force of our assailants should have assembled : but fortunately we had just time to sheer off, and were
swept close by a large fallen tree that had been washed down on

a sandbank, whose shadowy outline we had mistaken in the dark for the canoes of our enemies. Had we struck this obstacle we should inevitably have been capsized, and become a prey to the hordes of savages who were following us in their canoes, a few hundred yards astern ; for the darkness would then have rendered it almost impossible to repel an attack upon our undefended position. In the early hours of the morning, the war-horns, combined with the incessant beating of the drums and the savages' yells, kept us all on the alert. At daybreak numbers of armed natives were still following us in their canoes, but they kept well out of range, and merely scoffed and threatened us from a safe distance.

War-horns and drums continued to herald our approach from village to village, as we were borne rapidly onward by the swift current, but no further direct attempt was made to hinder our journey. A heavy storm came on at 9 A. M., and lasted until late in the afternoon, when we sighted a very large village on the left bank. The natives, who thronged the shore in dense masses, broke into indescribable excitement as we advanced, indulging in a series of frantic war-dances, and giving vent to loud cries, which echoed along the forest-clad banks and floated far out over the water. They manned their big war canoes, and their drums and ivory horns echoed for miles. They followed us for an hour to another large village, their weapons glistening in the sun, and their savage cries ringing in our ears. They kept out of range, however, and we sheered off behind an island just at the height of their excitement. The night was cloudy and we kept in midstream, but were saluted continually by the drum and horn alarms. All through the long night I kept watch, peering anxiously into the darkness. I knew not at what moment we might be attacked ; the drums and horns sounded from all sides and sometimes the shrieking voices of the savages fell so keenly on the ear that my men thought that the foe was upon them. I got a little sleep toward morning, as we passed down a long reach of swampy forest, undisturbed by savage war cries.

The following morning we came on three abandoned canoes drifting down stream ; the men, being scared, had taken to the bush at our approach. About 10 A. M. we sighted a large village on the right bank, and some fishermen answered our calls of peace in the Kibangi language. They said they belonged to the big village of Morunja. They were too afraid to approach us nearer than two hundred yards, but even the semblance of a friendly greeting was welcome after our recent experience.

At midday we met more fishing canoes, and passed another large village on the right bank. Here some armed natives, in big war canoes, came out to meet us, but kept at a respectful distance, dancing and throwing up water at us with their paddles in derision. They would not tell us their tribe, or the name of their village, but insisted upon calling us Arab plunderers, in spite of our pro-testations that we were friends and bound on a peaceful errand. Later on in the afternoon we paddled down close to a large village called "Dobbo." But the people were adverse to our landing. We, however, went alongside the perpendicular bank, and made fast to some of their canoes, which were attached to stakes at the water's edge, for we were anxious to purchase food. Our stock of provisions was by this time very low indeed. My men were really famished ; they said little and grumbled not at all, but their eyes had a starved look in them and they tightened their loin cloths day by day in a vain effort to stifle the pangs of hunger. In answer to our friendly overtures, the natives soon came in crowds around us, and on the river side their canoes hemmed us in, their occupants struggling to approach us, and anxious to exchange their bananas, fowls, bad eggs, sugar cane, small goats, dried fish,

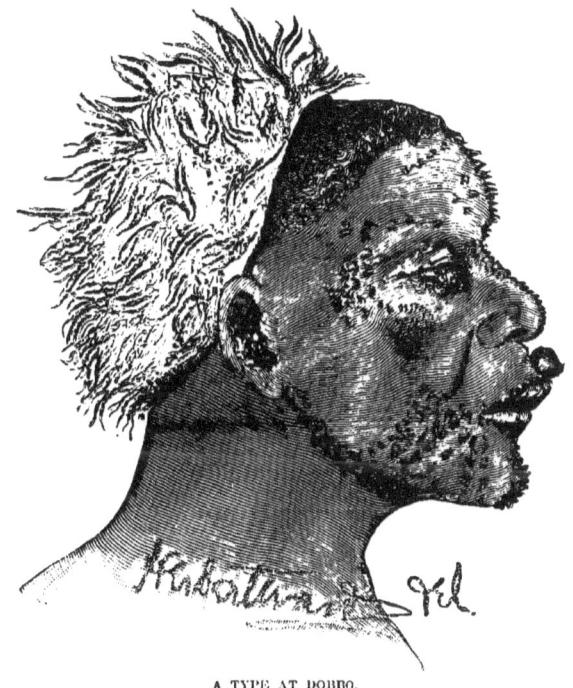

A TYPE AT DOBBO.

and other trifles, for beads, shells and empty cartridge cases; and so intense was their excitement, and so rough did their manner become, that I considered it advisable to depart before we came to blows.

As the course of the river changed from northwest to almost due west, it was apparent that we were approaching the populous and hostile district of Oupoto, where I feared we should have trouble. They had killed several State soldiers in a pitched battle with the Belgian chief of Bangala Station about a year before, and the Houssas who deserted my friend, Captain Deane, in his gallant fight against the Arabs at Stanley Falls, succeeded in passing all the other hostile places, but were captured by the Oupoto, who killed and ate five of them; the remainder were subsequently ransomed by the Congo State.

About 8 P. M. we took what appeared to be a clear reach of the river, but the night was so cloudy and dark that we had drifted down quite a distance into a narrow, reedy stretch of shoal water ere we discovered our error; and it was some time before we regained the proper channel.

At early dawn of the next morning we sighted the Oupoto Hills, and put into shore to get more firewood, as we had to abandon our stock last night in the swamp. Crowds of natives were excitedly skurrying about in the distance in their canoes. At about noon we responded to the earnest invitations of the natives, whose village on the south bank is nearly opposite Oupoto. These people, although they were very friendly, and sold all manner of food to the men—fish, fowl, plantain, kwanga—had stationed in the forest a party of armed warriors, ready to attack us at a moment's notice, in case of treachery on our part. The spears and knives of these men in ambush glistened in the bright sunlight as they peeped from behind the bushes. The villagers were very noisy and excited at seeing such a strange-looking craft as ours. My old green tent draped upon the framework of branches, with the two or three parrots we were bringing down perched solemnly on its summit, and the black, shaggy-tailed monkey I was carrying as a present to a friend at Stanley Pool,

sitting with a complacent smile in the bow, all combined to form
a novel picture in the eyes of these unsophisticated savages. But
all went well, and after about an hour's roaring, haggling, bartering and gesticulating in our negotiations for the purchase of food,
we went our way. As we shoved off I observed a knot of the
dusky beauties of the village whose artistic toilettes consisted only
of a necklace and a smile, on the principle, no doubt, that "beauty
unadorned is adorned the most," regarding us from the shelter of
a clump of banana trees "in maiden meditation, fancy free," and
wondering probably how a white man would taste. What with
whiffs of smoke, dried fish, high meat, sour manioc, and the
offensive odors of the other eatables which the men had invested
in. I could not enjoy much fresh air, so I smoked my pipe, and
contemplated the artless display of fast-fading loveliness on shore.

The heat was excessive, and I don't think an ordinary
thermometer could have registered the temperature without an
accident. We made good progress during the remainder of the
day ; saw but few natives in the distance, and passed down some
very narrow reaches among ugly snags. The night was uneventful ; it rained heavily in the early morning, but cleared off towards
noon, as, still keeping the north bank, we drifted through
channels between low, swampy islands. Nothing occurred until
about 3 P. M., when we met four naked natives in two canoes,
who told us that we could not get to Bangala until the next
morning, but they did not reckon on our going night and day.
They were very friendly, and accepted my little present of Kowrie
shells with evident satisfaction. They said their village was called
Ndubwa. I was able to chat with them in the Kibangi language.
Low-lying islands, clothed with dense jungles and forest, continue,
and the banks seem quite submerged.

In the night, about ten o'clock, we got into a narrow channel ; all was silent and dark, when several hippopotami rushed for the water from the narrow, reedy banks, where they had been dozing. Some almost rushed upon us in their efforts to gain the river, whilst the water surged and rolled about until I feared one of the monsters would take it into his head to charge us. Such an event would have been the end of our canoe journey. About midnight, as we passed some villages on the north bank, the alarm drums beat, and a very gruff voice challenged us.

" We are friends, children of Stanley, going to Bangala ; we are peaceable," said we. I told them we were Stanley's children, for Stanley's native name, Bula Matadi, " The Stonebreaker," acts as a talisman throughout the Congo country. By millions of these savages his name is uttered with respect almost akin to fear. It was evident that the natives did not believe our declaration, for the gruff voice replied :

"If you are what you say, why do you travel in the dark ? You lie, and we will come to you presently and fight, for you are like thieves, traveling in the dark."

We laughed at them, and went on, but the night was intensely dark, and being anxious lest we should miss the right channel, we made the canoes fast alongside the bank until daybreak ; passing the night without interruption from the natives—who, on reconsidering the matter, probably had believed our assurance that we were children of Stanley.

At very earliest streak of dawn on the following morning, we were off again, and passed many villages on the north bank that had grown up in the interval since my stay at Bangala in 1886.

After having been accustomed so long to the nude tribes of the upper region, it was pleasant to observe here the handsome forms of the women attired in their becoming, ballet-like grass skirts, dyed red, or brown, or black, according to the taste of the wearer, and to listen to their merry chaff as we floated past, and although they vied with each other in pressing invitations to land and indulge in friendly converse, we laughingly pleaded our haste as an excuse for not acceding to their kindly offers of hospitality.

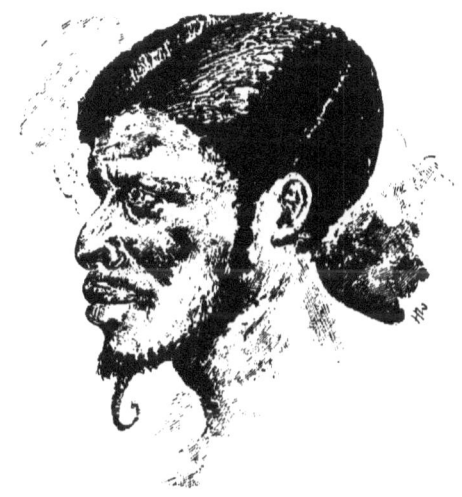

CHIEFTAIN OF BANGALA.

CHAPTER II.

My Soudanese officer dies—A tornado—"How many brass rods will you give me for two women to help paddle your canoe?"—My Wangwana's songs— Hippopotami—The Bateke or "Trading People."

ABU BAK, my Soudanese officer, who had been hopelessly ill with dysentery ever since our departure from Rachid's camp, grew daily worse, and now, terribly thin and unable to stand, was perfectly helpless. It was pleasing to watch the attention paid him by my four other Soudanese soldiers ; for, although they were the biggest ruffians and *cut-throats* one could meet with, yet they were as tender to poor old Abu Bak as any nurse. This attention on their part was due to Abu Bak's high Mahometan caste. Poor fellow ! he died the following morning in the arms of one of his countrymen, and was buried at Bangala, where we arrived late in the evening.

It is strange, when human beings are thrown together in some perilous enterprise in which the lives of all concerned are equally at stake, how differences of caste, color, and religion lose much of their power to divide and separate. A common interest unites natures the most diverse, and dangers faced side by side discover to the white man qualities and virtues in his humble, dusky follower, which he believed to be the choice product of his own civilization.

Poor Abu Bak was densely ignorant and superstitious. His morality was not of a high order, but according to his feeble lights he tried to do his duty, and he would without fear have given his life in a cause for which his limited intelligence could not have divined the reason or necessity.

There was great consternation among the Belgian officers of the Congo Free State Station, who at first, in the confusion attendant upon our sudden arrival, totally unexpected as it was, concluded we were a band of hostile Arabs. It was intensely dark, and in all probability we should have passed the station had it not been for the barking of a dog, which announced the presence of white men, as the native pariah dogs are only able to snarl, and never before had the harsh bark of a dog, abruptly breaking the silence of midnight, fallen on my ear with a sound so cheery and melodious.

At Bangala I found it necessary to change some of my Zanzibari crew, and replace them with natives of the district, who are renowned for their dexterity in managing a canoe. Upon quitting the station, my crew consisted of nine Zanzibaris and twelve men and four women, natives of Bangala, who only after much persuasion and some difficulty, consented to accompany me on such a long journey as that to Stanley Pool—a distance of about five hundred miles.

At midnight we were caught in a tropical tornado, and as our canoes possessed but little freeboard, we ran some danger of being swamped from the rapid rise of the miniature swell which accompanies these atmospheric outbreaks. Preceded by a dull, torpid calm, the heavy air breaks into no cooling breeze to fan the brows of the weary paddlers ; a deeper silence seems to settle down over river and forest-lined bank, affecting even the usually voluble Bangala women, and broken only now and then by some distant cry of a night bird from the forest depths, that well accords, in its plaintive, wailing monotony, with the sadness which seems to brood over the midnight river. A darker bank of cloud gathers from a corner of the heavens and spreads across the sky, shutting out stars and whatever hesitating light the moon may be striving to shed down upon us. Darker and stiller grows the scene, and our men hasten to gain the shelter of some overhanging bank, when, with a sudden flash, accompanied by a crashing peal that seems to split the sky right over our heads, the tornado bursts upon us, driving before it in swirling gusts the spray and foam of the brown river; to which is speedily added all the fury of a tropical rainfall. Perfect cataracts of water descend; the roar of the wind, uprooting here a tree weakened through age, and tearing off sturdy branches, is heard in the forest, even amid the crashing peals of thunder which follow each other in rapid succession. No one attempts to speak; " in solemn silence all," each regards his neighbor's face, lit up and livid from the ghastly glare of the lightning flash. Huddled together for warmth beneath the cold and pitiless down pour, the men await the termination of the storm. In ten minutes, peace, and a tranquil, starlit sky, succeed to the darkness and fury we have just experienced; a cooling breeze springs up, and we hear the rushing of the water in the channels among the trees pouring over the banks of the Congo The canoes are bailed out; the monkey and the half-drowned parrots emerge from their retreat beneath my sadly tumbled tent; there is wringing out of drenched garments on the part of the men, and after a few minutes, laughter and chatter take the place of the late silence, and we proceed once more on our way.

At about 3 A. M. we struck a big snag, and had considerable difficulty in getting off again. At 2 P. M. we reached the mouth of the Lulanga River, and my people exchanged chaff with the hordes of natives who thronged the banks of the river.

The Lulanga here enters the Congo. It is probably a mile in width, and comes from the land of the Balolo, or "Iron People," skilled in the manufacture of arms. At its junction with the Congo, the left bank is dotted for miles with the round-roofed houses embowered in the leafy shade of rich banana and plantain groves—the agglomeration of villages known as Lulanga town to the traders and State officials.

A few hours afterwards, about eight canoes came out to us with armed men, who made a speech, the purport of which was that we were not welcome, and that if we did not keep our eyes open something might happen. We laughed at them, showed our guns, and ended by exchanging small presents.

The evening was balmy and pleasant ; the droning chant of my Wangwanas (free-men—a name by which the men of Zanzibar are commonly known), and the measured dip of their paddles, appropriately suited the situation. I slept fitfully, in a sitting posture, but had to remain awake more or less all night, on account of the hippopotami that continually rose up all around us, necessitating careful steering on our part to avoid coming in contact with the huge monsters.

The sunset that evening was gorgeous. The rolling tide of the river, ebbing away before us to the westward, which all day had reflected the dazzling light of the blue sky overhead, and had been a pain to the eyes to look at, now assumed a sadder, softer tinge, a light, pearly gray, later on tipped every ripple with flashes of crimson and gold, and then all blazed out into a perfect sea of color, as the sun swiftly shot behind the line of dark forest trees that cut the sky line. Then, as night rapidly climbed up the eastern sky, the forest trees stood out dark and bold, a serrated crown of waving palm and mighty cotton trees—against the shifting, changing colors of the sky in the background—a mass of every hue of crimson and red—from darkest orange to softest pink, gradually fading upward into an opal-green tinge, which again became merged in the advancing darkness of night.

We went along very fairly until about midnight, when we got into an intricate back-water. From midnight until after 5 A. M., we were lost in this maze of channels, with banks of long swamp grass and thick forests. At last I hailed a fishing canoe, and got on the right track. The people seemed mystified as to who we were. At 7. 30 I saw three big buffaloes about a mile off, but I couldn't manage to hunt them, as the swamp was too deep, and only a strong animal could force its way through the grass. It seemed quite ludicrous that during the day we could follow the proper channel without the least difficulty, but as soon as night came on we frequently got into some blind pool or back water, or ran into the bank, where the prickly bushes tore our clothes and flesh.

"How many brass rods will you give me for these two women to help paddle your canoe down to Busindi?" asked a man in the canoe that put us on the right track this morning. This he said in a jeering tone, to express his contempt for our awkwardness in paddling.

I staid at the large village of Busindi for an hour, buying fowls, kwanga (boiled cassava) sugar-cane, and manioc, for which I gave brass wire, empty bottles, tins, iron spoons and Kowrie shells. The chief gave me a fine big duck, and some eggs, but he who accepts presents from the dusky potentates of Central Africa, might say with Virgil, "*Timeo Danaos et dona ferentes,*" and, alas! in the present instance, I found the chief's intentions were better than his eggs, for they proved all bad—these eggs so eagerly desired, and so heavily paid for, when the value of my return present came to be considered. The duck, which I had carefully broiled on a stick, proved excessively tough ; I had no bread nor salt—but what matter?—it was a duck. In the morning as we drifted along I tried to shave in the drizzling rain, and gashed my chin badly. My little mirror being cracked across the middle, I could only see the lower part of my face in two hemispheres.

This attempt afforded great amusement to the Bangala women, who broke out into further peals of merriment at the sight of my tooth-brush and comb, and my efforts to part my hair.

About midnight a strong squall came up the river, and nearly swamped us before we could reach the bank. We bailed out the water with a bucket, and remained weather-bound for several hours. We paddled on with much difficulty, and at last reached the Baptist Mission Station at Lukolela, where I was kindly received by Darby and Harrison, two young English missionaries.

As the cool air of approaching night braces up the Bangalas, they sing a livelier refrain, and bend their backs, their paddles sending the spray flying up astern. As the moon rises, the bold Wangwanas are at the paddles, singing their musical chants of Arabic origin, "Sudi Mtumwa Leo" (Sudi is a Slave to-day) and "Karatas ana Wino" (Paper and Ink).

The next morning I was up long before dawn, cheering on the men. We made good progress, and at 7 A. M. came to a long reach where the hippopotami evidently breed, for we were in the midst of at least a hundred. One rose up at about two or three feet from the canoe, and splashed the muddy water over us. His great jaws were open, displaying his gleaming tusks, which would have made short work of any occupant of our canoes unfortunate enough to have placed himself inconveniently near the brute. In-

deed, I couldn't help thinking that if a noted Irishman once
declared his ability to drive a coach and six through an act of
Parliament, our steersman might, by an unlucky turn of his guid-
ing paddle, have sent a canoe and twelve through the jaws of this
hippo!

We had not traveled far when from a quiet stretch of river
under the lee of a grass covered sandbank, protruded the solitary
head of another of these monsters. This fellow, either resenting
our presence in what he probably chose to consider his own private demesne, or more likely being one of those surly bulls too ill-
tempered to herd with the rest, came right at us with open jaws.
I feared we were in for worse than a mere ducking this time, and
so evidently thought my men, for most of them jumped headlong
into the water and made for the shore. The shock knocked me
down, and I injured my arm as I fell with it doubled under me,
while Msa (my Zanzibari servant) got a bad cut over the eye from
my boot as I fell. The brute smashed a great lump off the stern
of the biggest canoe, and carried away all the lashings. I was
expecting he would come again, but he made off with a deal of
fuss, splashing the water around him into foam. Msa's eye I
dressed with vinegar, no other medicines being at hand. Not that
I considered vinegar was any good for such a wound, but negroes
have a habit of gauging the strength of medicine by the amount of
pain it causes. I picked a piece of the hippo's tusk out of the
broken stern of the canoe, which we had to patch with clay.

A number of canoes filled with Bateke people, and laden with
peanuts and corn, passed us going up the river, hugging the shore.
They looked upon us with suspicion, and would say nothing. The
Bangalas chaffed them, as we passed, and would end with a derisive howl, significant of their contempt for men who are only fit

to buy and sell, the Bateke being, as their name signifies, literally, "the Trading People." Being the great trading community of the Lower Congo, situated at Stanley Pool, their position as traders is a naturally good one, and they have not been slow to avail themselves of it. They have constituted themselves the middle-men between the ivory-trading tribes from the Upper Congo and the Bakongo of the Lower River, and reap substantial profits as the result of their self-imposed mediation.

The elevated position of all the Bolobo villages presents a strong contrast to the country further to the eastward. I understand that Mr. Grenfell, the English Baptist missionary, is about to reside here. He is quite the best man I know for such a place, but

RIVER SCENE AT BOLOBO.

I cannot help feeling that the trading disposition is too strongly ingrained in the people for a missionary to cause any speedy reformation in their lives. The condition of the Congo native, after putting aside his chances of being murdered and eaten, or taken as a slave, is greatly superior to that of the poorer classes in some parts of the civilized world. His wants are few, and they are easily satisfied, with slight physical effort. Fish abound in the rivers ; game can be trapped in the forest ; all the necessary materials for hut-building and canoe-making are at hand. A genial sun shines upon him daily, and at night he coils around his fire in the hut, with no care for the morrow's victuals

and no heart-breaking prospect of misery in the coming winter
for want of meat and shelter.

We have just had another smash from a hippopotamus. We
saw the creature ahead, and I told the men to sheer off, but they
had not time, and in another instant the sterns of both canoes
were high in the air, and most of my men were sent flying into
the water. A little of this sort of thing is not bad fun, but we
did not want any more trifling from hippopotami. We again had
to stop and repair the broken lashings. If the canoes had been
smashed the last time, I doubt if any of us would have been powerful swimmers enough to reach the shore, for we were a long
way out in the river, the current was strong, and crocodiles
abounded, ever ready for a meal. I have often been among hippopotami in a small dug-out, shooting them right and left, but was
never attacked before as I had been during this journey. However, all's well that ends well, and we recovered from this assault
as from the previous one, and from this point were enabled to
pursue our journey in peace and safety.

CHAPTER III.

We ship a passenger—Lone Island of Chumbiri—Interrupt an elephant at breakfast—We enter Stanley Pool—Lost in a maze of sand-banks—A narrow escape.

THE estimated population of the Bolobo district is thirty thousand. The people are robust, and the country around is highly fertile. It was the dry season when I passed, and the tints marking the recent bush and grass fires were rich in browns and reds, as the ruddy light of the setting sun lit up the vast expanse of water, and the high, forested hills in the distance; the roofs of the natives' huts in the villages climbing the tree-clad sides, or crowning the otherwise bare summits of the north bank range, or nestling amid a bower of thick palm and banana foliage at the water's edge, and the irregular, bright green patches of cultivation, showing from out the forest clearings, all combined to produce a harmony of color and diversity of outline charming to the eye after the monotony of the league-long stretches of low-lying, swampy bank, with its interminable barrier of forest, of the Upper River.

Several canoe loads of Bolobo natives passed us on their way to visit some neighboring villages, their occupants singing joyously some local canoe song, no doubt relying upon the many pots of ardent "malafu" they carried with them to insure a hearty welcome. This beverage, when freshly drawn from the palm-tree, at either early morning or just before sunset, is an invigorating and a scarcely intoxicating draught. But, on being left to stand in the sun some little time, it speedily ferments and forms a somewhat "heady" and exhilarating tipple, in which form it never fails to play an important part in all Congo concerns, whether domestic or public. To its influence the tardy orator owes the increased fluency and vigor of utterance which enables him to carry his point at the "palaver" gathering. The warrior, ere departing to the scene of strife, grasps, it is true, his spear and shield with one hand, but in the other the neck of a gourd, bubbling and foaming with this insidious liquor; and when victory crowns his efforts, he ascribes, I have no doubt, the success of his arms as much to the potent effects of the "malafu" he has drunk as to the aid of any guardian "fetich" or evil spirit—for he fails not, on his safe return, to sacrifice to Bacchus with copious libations, ere ascribing honor elsewhere, or acknowledging assistance from any other source.

We pursued our way, my men responding to the friendly greetings we encountered; the "Omwa" and "Omwa-na-yo" ("good-mornings" and "good mornings to you, too") passing from canoe to canoe in amicable interchange of civilities.

Towards midnight the wind arose, and the water becoming too rough for us to proceed, we sought shelter for the night in some swamp grass. The following morning we started off again, but soon found farther progress impossible, owing to the strength of the wind blowing right up river in our faces; however, about noon, the cessation of the breeze rendered the resumption of our journey once more practicable, and we were again steering out into mid stream, to gain the advantage of the increased current in the main channel of the river. The heat became intense now that the wind had dropped, and the glaring light reflected from the water was most trying to our eyes.

In the afternoon, as we drifted past the upper village of Chumbiri, a native waded up to his waist in the river, beckoning us ashore. He said that he had plenty of bananas, fowls and malafu for sale, but they were in a village a little lower down; however, he would accompany us, and as a guarantee of good faith, he placed his "fetich" and "charms" in the canoe, while he went away to get his spears.

NEAR CHUMBIRI.

Upon starting, a woman rushed to the beach and tried to prevent his departure, and, indeed, he had to use force to keep her out of the canoe. The poor woman said nothing, but there was an expression of suppressed grief upon her countenance as she waded along the shore up to her shoulders in the water. All the village people, meanwhile, cried out to her in alarm, lest she should be snapped up by a crocodile. She followed over the big boulders and forced her way through the long swamp grass along the river bank, for a considerable distance, occasionally wringing her hands, but without saying a word.

What this domestic strife meant I could not conceive, unless, perhaps, she was jealous of her husband accompanying me to another village where some rival beauty might reside. Some time afterwards the man indicated a spot where we should run the canoes into shore. Carefully gathering up his charms, he stepped out on to the bank and was making off without a word.

"Where's the malafu, the fowls, and the other food you promised to sell us?" I cried.

He replied that he had none, and that he only wanted a passage down the river into another district, for he was a prisoner of war and they had allowed him to enter my canoe without obstruction for fear of giving me offence. The woman was a fellow-prisoner who had been threatened with death should this man escape; but I had reason to doubt the truth of this portion of his story, seeing the freedom of movement permitted her in following up the canoe so long, and I was led to hope that, perhaps, a kindlier fate might be reserved for her.

Below Chumbiri the aspect of the country changes and the scenery is very beautiful. From the Lone Island, standing like a sentinel, in mid-stream, opposite Chumbiri, guarding the approach to the mysterious realm of swamps and forests, of wild, cannibal savages and dark deeds of pitiless cruelty wrought in their midst —a land which here may be said to take its beginning—up to the mouth of the Aruimi tributary, the Congo flows through a broad channel between low-lying banks, its surface dotted with islands innumerable, that break up the course of navigation and render it impossible to say whether the land seen on right hand or left is mainland or island, so intricate is the net-work of channels by which the river flows through this vast assemblage of islands, and so similar in appearance is the vegetation that clothes them to that lining the true banks of the stream. It is only at two or three places that, in all this long extent of waterway, the two shores of the river become visible at the same point, unobstructed by intervening land; but the Lone Island of Chumbiri marks the termination of this long series of interruptions to the view and to navigation at the same time.

Below it the river is unrolled in all its majestic proportions, its shining, silvery surface unbroken over all its breadth from shore to shore, save by the passing canoe of some fisherman seeking the shallows where he can spread his nets, or the larger craft of the Byanzi traders, propelled down mid-stream in the full force of the current by the strong arms of the slaves of some Bolobo chief, descending to sell his tusks of ivory to the Bateke middle-men around the shores of Stanley Pool. The rich voices of the slaves ring out over the waters, as they chant, in time to the swift stroke of their paddles, some flattering eulogy of their master, or recital of their prowess in the field of Cupid or of Mars ; a track of foam and ripples closing in the wake of their canoe, as its prow dashes aside the brown waters of the river.

Rising from each bank, in swelling shoulders of rich green in the early rains, changing to brown and red as the season advances, until the grass-fires consume the herbage in the dry months of July and August, are the hills of the Byanzi's on the south and Bateke on the north—a kindred tribe to that surrounding Stanley Pool. These hills attain an altitude of from 500 feet to 600 feet above the surface of the river, rising near Stanley Pool to a height of probably 1000 feet. Their summits are rounded and covered with grass alone, while the lower stretches are hidden in climbing groves of the richest tropical vegetation. The broad leaves of the *pandanus* mingle with the graceful fronds of the oil-palm, or are half smothered in the clinging embrace of the tree-fern, or by the innumerable tendrils of the vines and creepers, which, rope-like, festoon the trunks of the trees, and extend their graceful arms from branch to branch, until, gaining the summit and finding no further resting-place beyond, they fall back upon themselves, and form a hanging crown of verdure and bright blossoms, overshadowing the trees that support them. Soaring high above all this leafy confusion, and extending their wide arms, unimpeded by a rival's, into the serene air, the cotton-trees (the *bombax* of the botanist) hang their snowy bunches above the topmost palm tree's summit, and rivet the eye by the magnificence of their bulk and the fresh green of their foliage.

Idly drifting down the stream—for our progress in so unwieldy a craft depended more upon the will of the current than our own exertions—I allowed my eye to rest upon this scene with singular pleasure, and a sense of dreamy contentment stole over me after my recent experiences amid the winding channels and long, uninteresting reaches of the upper river; uninteresting to the eye in their monotonous sameness, yet at times their passage rendered thrillingly exciting by the wild rush of savages in their war-canoes round some unexpected point, or by the deep, hoarse cries echoing along their banks, and the booming of the drums which announced our approach to enemies lurking in some covert below. Here no such surprises were in store for us; the rocky banks and tree-hidden bays concealed no worse foe than the keen Bateke or Byanzi trader, thirsting, not for the white man's blood, but for his cotton cloths and bright brass rods, and anxious only to get the better of him in bargaining, when his natural timidity and suspicion had been lulled to sleep by the exhibition of such " unconsidered trifles " of this description as my fast-failing and scanty stock enabled me to display, whenever my own wants or the necessities of my men induced us to call at any of the villages we might pass.

I was glad to feel this ease of mind and freedom from harassing dread of attack ; and looking up stream, the Lone Island of Chumbiri had ceased to show out against the sky-line, reminding me of what lay beyond the islands that commence at that solitary rock.

There were many grass fires in different directions, and the blue and white smoke hanging over the hills, tinged with the warm red light of the setting sun, made a striking picture. The night passed without incident, but at daylight we came suddenly upon a big bull elephant that was feeding on the tender young grass at the water's edge. His long tusks were beautifully white, and his great ears flapped lazily as he pulled up tufts of the succulent grass with his trunk. Hastily snatching up my rifle, I landed as noiselessly as possible, but unfortunately, before I could gain a point from which to deliver a telling shot, he got our wind and stalked away into the dense forest. I followed him for a considerable distance through the woods without success.

We passed the mouth of the Kasai River a few hours later. The sun was terrifically hot, and my men showed evident signs of fatigue from want of sleep. The next day the water was very rough, and we had several narrow escapes from being swamped. Our progress, drifting with the current, was counteracted by the strong head wind blowing with much violence up the gorge through which the river here flows. Five of my people were lying in the bottom of the canoes suffering from fever, and I was without medicine to alleviate their pain. We entered Stanley Pool shortly after noon, and by sundown we were picking our way in shallow water among a maze of sand-banks. In addition to the dense darkness which followed sunset, we were enveloped in a thick fog, and were unable to distinguish any landmark. We soon found ourselves in deep water, being carried along by the swift current. We could distinctly hear the roar of the cataracts in the distance.

The low, booming sound echoing through the starless night, growing instantly more and more distinct, brought with it a message, the dread purport of which was depicted on every anxious face.

THE BANGALA WOMEN CRY AND WRING THEIR HANDS

For a while not a word was spoken, but a sense of that tense expectancy felt when life is risked at long odds was present to all.

Our situation was critical, and we strained every muscle to reach the bank. Owing, however, to the density of the fog, we could distinguish nothing ; we could not even discern a star to steer by, and, in the meanwhile, the ominous roar of the cataracts

CATARACTS OF THE CONGO.

grew louder and louder, causing the Bangala women to cry and wring their hands, saying :

"Our friends told us of the danger of this journey ; why did we leave our homes to be drowned in the cataracts of Ntamo ? [the name by which the upper river people call Stanley Pool]   O ! mam-a-a, mam-a-a !"

The men were silent, and paddled with all their remaining

strength. Every now and then the haft of a paddle would snap. At last the Zanzibaris commenced muttering to themselves in piteous tones :

"Allah, Il Allah ! Mahomed Il-Sura-Allah !" And my faithful servant, Msa, said : "Eh Bwana wangu. Tu-ta kufa leo." (Oh, my master, we shall all die.)

We were almost at our wit's end, for we could see no land to steer for ; and we were being swept down by the fierce current towards the cataracts, which we estimated, by the distinctness of their roar, could not be many miles off. Some of the men sank down in the bottom of the canoes, exhausted and in despair : when happily a breeze sprang up, and as the fog cleared away we could distinguish the low forest bank of Ndolo, just above the dangerous, rocky islands of Kinchassa. We now paddled with renewed vigor, and by daylight reached our destination, Leopold-ville Station, at the lower end of Stanley Pool.

CHAPTER IV.

Return to Stanley Falls—Interesting afternoon chats—Adventure with a snake—A friend of Dr. Livingstone's—I am accused of blasphemy—A tropical thunderstorm.

A FTER journeying to the coast, I returned a few months later to Stanley Pool, where I embarked on board a steam-launch belonging to the government of the Congo Free State, bound for Stanley Falls, on arriving at which station I took up my abode with the Arabs during the few weeks of my stay.

Sitting among the Arabs, in their snowy robes, turbans, and gold and silver-braided waistcoats, with all their attention riveted upon me, was a novel experience, and one full of interest.

I had to enter into minute detailed descriptions of the ways and customs of my countrymen in far-off Europe, as the coffee, handed round in little china cups, poured from a long-necked Arabic coffee-pot, induced that spirit of inquiry and reply which civilized ladies enjoy over their cups of afternoon tea under the name of gossip. I was requested to give a brief historical outline of the famous wars of Napoleon Bonaparte, and of his victorious marches through conquered Europe, rivaling the achievements of Timour or Genghis Kahn of old. This was a subject that interested the Arabs deeply, and I was frequently interrupted by questions regarding the action and pattern of the rifles used by the soldiers of that time, of the earthworks they attacked and defended, and of the modes of transport employed in moving their trains of artillery and heavy siege guns. Then that subject was abruptly changed, and I was forced into a complicated explanation concerning the manufacture of cotton cloth at Manchester. Changing again as abruptly, I was closely interrogated as to administration and political organization in Turkey, or requested to describe the personal peculiarities of his majesty the Sultan. Then an old Arab, whose face was deeply wrinkled and sun-burned from years of privation and the exposure of African travel, said :

TIPPO TIB'S HOUSE AT STANLEY FALLS.

"Would twenty thousand dollars be sufficient money for me to travel through Europe with, and see all these wonderful things you have told us of ? And how should I find the road ? For there must be many paths through the different countries of Europe."

Each morning my little clay hut was crowded with noisy, foul-smelling savages of the Lokeri tribe, in all their most fashionable feather head-dresses and war paint, for I used to send to the village for these men in order that I might make typical drawings, some of which illustrate this book.

One evening I went to the river to swim, and when about twenty yards from the shore, one of my Zanzibaris on the bank shouted out : "Nyoka! Nyoka! Bwana!" (Snake, snake, master!) And looking around, I found, sure enough, there was a snake within a few feet, swimming towards me. The current was strong, and it was only after the greatest exertion I just managed to reach the bank in time to escape from a black, venomous snake several feet long.

Early one morning I found a poor, wretched youth, a native of some far country, brought as a slave by the Arabs, lying stretched

on the rocks in a dying condition. Every bone of his body was visible, and his skin had assumed a gray hue, and was deeply wrinkled. I sent him food and had him carried to shelter, but he was too far gone, and died a few hours afterwards.

The white man can never, as long as he may live in Africa, conquer his repugnance to the callous indifference to suffering that he meets with everywhere in Arab and Negro. The dying are left by the wayside to die. The weak drop on the caravan road, and the caravan passes on. Life is for the strong and the powerful, and the slave —well, perhaps he is fortunate if left undisturbed

WOMAN WITH BURDEN.

to await death, which brings to him freedom from countless miseries.

MY HUT AT STANLEY FALLS

Amid such incidents as these the time slipped away, and it became necessary for me to again make preparations for my second long journey down to the Atlantic coast ; and on the eve of my departure several Arabs came to my little hut camp to bid me farewell.

Among them was old Mohammed Bin Seid, familiarly known

VIEW ON
THE LOMANI RIVER.

to the Arabs as "Bwana Makubwa" (The Reverend). He was a perfect gentleman in his manner, and so kind-hearted that the other Arabs frequently ridiculed him for his generosity to his slaves. He had been particularly kind and hospitable to me when I visited his country several months previously. He was bowed down with age, and as he tremblingly took my hand, he said :

"Kwaheri rafiki angu," (Good-bye, my friend). Adding : "You are a young man, going to your country far away. I am old, and will soon pass away here in the desert. I knew old Daod Lifeston (Dr. David Livingstone) at Tabora. He was a good old man. We all liked his kindly manner. How loose his teeth were from age ! They rattled like the castanets our women play. But they boiled his meat soft. He was a great man among white men, was he not ? We shall not meet again ; so good bye."

And the old man, in his picturesque robes of snowy whiteness, went his way.

The following day, at noon, I embarked in two large canoes, lashed together side by side. I had with me ten Zanzibaris, two Niam-Niams, (natives of the Upper Welle country, who had been captured during some Arab raid, but proving of no service to their captors from their weakness and stupidity, I obtained possession of them, intending to take them down to one of the Baptist mission stations on the Lower River, where they might recover strength and intelligence under kindly treatment,) and seven Manyemas, who had just returned from a long journey through the country of the Dwarfs. Tippo Tib and his suite came down to the banks of the river to bid me a last farewell, and Tippo Tib advised me to reconsider my plans ; for he said my force was absurdly inadequate to cope with the hordes of savage cannibals about the Aruimi. I called his attention to my cases of ammunition. He smiled, and shrugging his shoulders, said :

"You may consider yourself well armed, but what can you do against such numbers ?"

An hour later we were under way, drifting down the Congo with a two knot current. We passed by several large villages, all of which were under the Arab's sway. Towards the evening the sky grew cloudy, and we experienced a terrific thunderstorm. The united efforts of several men were necessary to bail out the water to keep us afloat; by midnight we reached the camp of Abdallah Ngaziga. All was darkness, and we made fast our canoes until daylight, when the aston-ished Abdallah came hurry-ing down to the beach, ac-companied by several slaves, carrying presents of sweet potatoes, sugar-cane, plan-tains, and a cooked breakfast of curried fowl, eggs, molas-ses and rice, and also a big black monkey, a species of Chimpanzee, which walked down the hill hand in hand with a little slave boy, and my acceptance of which the hospitable Arab entreated as a favor. I smiled, thinking of the poor time of it the other monkey had had during my first journey.

Proceeding on again, we drifted past several more large native villages. The savages, however, took but

little notice of us, as they supposed we were Arabs. At noon the
heat was intense, and we were disagreeably crowded together in
the narrow canoes. The fowls would flutter and clatter in their
captivity, my two goats bleated most piteously, and added to the
prevailing discomfort by their efforts to escape from the rays of
the sun. The Zanzibaris paddled lazily, and droning the while a
sad, monotonous chant. The Manyemas alternately chattered and
ate sugar-cane, while the Niam-Niams solemnly, and at regular
intervals, scooped up the bilge water in an old earthen cooking
pot.

Towards sunset we reached the populous village of Yalisula,
which is ruled by Saidi, a minion of the Arabs, with a few Manyemas as body guard. I produced some brass wire and red cloth,
to purchase curiosities and weapons from the natives. They grew
frantic at the sight of such wealth, and hurriedly brought every
conceivable article they could lay their hands upon ; old broken
wooden stools, fish skulls, necklaces of antelopes' teeth, cam-wood,
palm-oil, bad eggs, shields, spears, skinny fowls, arrows and
knives. Upon asking them to sell some of their necklaces of human teeth, which are quite fashionable in these cannibal countries,
they howled and danced, and several men rushed off to procure
some. A few minutes later, a big, burly savage forced his way
through the crowd, holding a long, fanged tooth covered with
blood. I asked what he thought I wanted one single tooth for ;
he replied that he must have misunderstood me ; he thought I
wanted to buy teeth, and as this tooth had pained him for several
days, he had pulled it out and brought it to me to sell!

I slept that night in my canoe, and was frequently awakened
by the noisy songs of the fishermen who continually passed and
re-passed in their huge canoes, which are hewn out of solid trees,

and are capable of holding fifty to sixty men in each. Leaving Saidi, the next morning at dawn, we continued our journey, drifting with the current until about noon we sighted a big canoe with a white canvas awning, propelled by a number of

native paddlers. I put into a little village close by, and awaited its arrival. Then out stepped the stately Rachid bin Mohammed bin Seid bin Hamad

"I SLEPT THAT NIGHT IN MY CANOE."

Marajib. He courteously invited me to visit his camp at the mouth of the Lomani, situated only a short distance further down the river. He sent on his own canoe and returned with me, augmenting my paddling force with twelve stalwart natives, whilst two other big canoes were lashed on either side of us, making quite a formidable flotilla ; they had two big drums, and singing a weird, deafening dirge, we proceeded down to the Lomani River.

The natives appeared to grow quite intoxicated in the heat of the sun, which was intense ; their faces were deeply scarred by cicatrization, giving the appearance of being covered with a mass of exaggerated pimples. Their upper lips were pierced, and circular pieces of ivory about an inch in diameter and half an inch thick, were inserted, and as they laughed and sang, and their mouths expanded, their black, filed teeth, and discolored gums were left bare. It is the custom of most cannibal tribes to file the front teeth to a point, and as the enamel is destroyed in the process, the teeth become black and the result is disgusting.

Upon reaching Rachid's camp, I was ushered into the mysterious interior of his seraglio, where the ladies of his harem resided. I spent the afternoon with Rachid, discussing the merits of Islamism. Rachid was a young and typical Mohammedan. He was third in command to Tippo Tib, and a slave-trader; but he was very devout, and went through all his devotions with scrupulous fidelity. He was well up in Mohammedan theology, and could recite the

A NATIVE VILLAGE.

Koran from end to end. He had but a vague idea of Christianity, and asked me what the fundamental tenets of our religion were. I replied that Christianity is founded on the belief that Jesus Christ is the Son of God. Rachid was terribly shocked at this declaration. He arose, folded his hands across his breast, bowed his head, and said, with impressive solemnity:

"We are friends, and I enjoy our conversations. You are welcome to my house and to everything I have, while you are my guest; but do not utter, in my presence, such blasphemy."

Rachid resumed his seat, and we changed the conversation. The time passed rapidly, and at sundown Rachid went to his devo- tions, and I retired soon afterwards to my canoes. A heavy thunderstorm came on at midnight, blowing away my awning, and literally drenching everything. Natives frequently passed in the night, beating drums and singing. There was a most offensive odor from the beach, where hundreds of natives were living in their light crafts, drawn up at the water's edge. These canoe dwellers had been so continually persecuted by the Arab's followers whilst residing in their villages, that they had taken to the water, so as to be ready at a moment's notice to escape from any threat- ening danger.

Every baby in the colony seemed to squall that night for my special benefit. The next morning, while I was engaged by gesture in negotiating for the purchase of a carved canoe paddle, offering in exchange an empty white glass vinegar bottle, the transparency of which, enabling the possessor to mark the fluctu- ations of the liquor it contained and to regulate the duration of his potations accordingly, rendered it an object greedily desired by all savage Africans. An Arab, who was standing by, said :

"It is difficult to understand these people with those lumps of ivory in their upper lips ; it makes their words tough."

From the Lomani River we drifted slowly along a line of vil- lages. It was market day on shore, and in canoes along the beach were congregated about three thousand savages engaged in buy- ing and selling native produce, fish and slaves. We passed about fifty yards out in the river, and the dull roar of their deep voices, engaged in argument, entreaty and expostulation, seemed to shake the air with vibration.

At the last village of the Arab territory on the south bank, I stopped, and, observing the chief was of a particularly picturesque appearance, I beckoned him into the drum house, sat down and drew his portrait. Hundreds of people crowded around us, almost excluding all air and light, but not a sound did they utter. Immediately after sketching the chief's portrait I embarked, and left without a word, to the surprise and intense mirth of the savage multitude, who had continually poured in from their adjacent huts to see the strange white man.

It seemed to tickle them greatly, this strange action of mine—first inviting their chief to be seated, then sitting opposite him for some time without opening my lips, and engaged all the while on what, to them, appeared to be something very trivial, and, finally, when they all thought the critical moment had arrived, and I had risen to address them, coolly walking away without so much as a parting word.

As they realized that I had "done" them in some way or other unknown to themselves, their wonder at myself and movements gave place to a burst of merriment, and chief and all shook with laughter.

This was the last of the friendly villages subjugated by the Arabs ; and from this on down to Oupoto I might expect a repetition of the suspicions exhibited by all on the occasion of my first journey, and of the covert attempts to attack us at night or overwhelm us in the daytime, that had rendered the passing of this long stretch of river a matter of anxiety and dread, when not even of actual danger.

CHAPTER V.

WE ARE CHALLENGED TO FIGHT—"YOU LIE, YOU ARE ARABS"—THE SAVAGE MONTS-
GERI—CHARRED HUTS AND DESOLATION—"GO AWAY! GO AWAY!"

WE continued our steady course as the sun set, but it was not until midnight that we again came upon evidences of life.

Suddenly, as we drifted past the lower end of a thickly wooded island, we encountered several canoes filled with armed men, whose spears and knives flashed in the bright moonlight. They howled at us with rage. Following us until dawn the next morning, they continued their war cry, which was a peculiar rattle of the throat, alternating with a falsetto scream. We passed the mouth of the Aruimi River the next morning about nine o'clock, in a blinding thunderstorm, which probably sheltered us from the savage Basoko. During the day we only sighted a few natives in canoes, who hurried off in frantic haste in all directions at our approach, and during the following night war-drums beat incessantly along the river banks, calling the people together and warning them of approaching danger.

At sunrise we sighted a village on the north bank, and as we drew near the natives gave the warning cry, like a cock crowing, indicating that the Arabs were coming to attack them, for, unfortunately, we were mistaken, as heretofore, for Arab slavers. As we approached, the men's gruff voices were raised in great excitement, and the women uttered piercing screams as they snatched up their children and rushed to the shelter of the forest.

As we passed, we could clearly distinguish the feather head-dresses of the men, as they moved about in hiding behind the broad-leaved banana trees lining the top of the bank, and tufts of jungle grass rankly sprouting from the water's edge. Here and there some savage, braver than the rest, stood alone with his spears and shield, ready for any emergency, either to fight or to run away. One man rushed forward to pick up his little pariah dog, and ran with it under his arm into the forest, lest we should be tempted to steal this dainty morsel; for dog's meat, in these cannibal countries, is highly esteemed; and, unlike the natives of the Lower Congo, who never feed their dogs, observing that the dog unable to find his food is not worth feeding and only fit to starve, these people fatten up and prize their dogs as second only to human flesh. Some hundreds of natives were assembled together in the distance, in their canoes. As we passed the village, the people rushed to the banks, seemingly surprised that we had not attacked them, and the voices of the men reached us, crying:

"Samba! samba! sen-nen-nen-na, sen nen na, kenda mboli sen-nen-nen-na!" (Good, good; it is well, it is well; go far away, and it is well;") and floating and paddling steadily on we were soon beyond the sound of their voices, and had removed from their minds the impression that we were going to attack them. We, of course, by our appearance, were everywhere mistaken for Arabs, and such an event as our passing by their village without looting or attempting to catch any people, would be the chief topic of conversation in those villages for many a day to come.

Later on we passed several war-canoes in the distance. They would not even answer our salutation—a bad sign. At length, one war-canoe, containing about fifty armed men, waited for us on the opposite bank of an island. As we drew near, the chief, whose bright iron bracelets and anklets glittered in the sunlight, made a long speech in a low, angry voice. He challenged us to fight, and warned us that we must sleep to-night with our eyes and ears open, or perhaps we should not see the morrow. Had they attacked us in numbers, we must assuredly have been beaten, and a cannibal orgy on our remains would have been the inevitable result ; for with so few men, none of whom I could depend upon, we could have only expected to hold out for a few hours ; their numbers must eventually have prevailed.

It was fortunate that the natives did not view the matter in the same light ; they were either daunted by the sight of the shining barrels of our rifles protruding over the gunwales of the

"ENJOYING THE SOLITUDE OF THE RIVER."

canoes, knowing the terrible power of destruction wielded by those silent metal tubes, or they were themselves so thankful at not having been called upon to resist an attack from us, the fear of which, no doubt, had first called them out in their numbers, that they permitted us to drift past them unmolested. Perhaps, too, a lurking suspicion that I *might* after all be what I proclaimed myself, a white man, prevented an open attack being made upon us. At any rate, I drew a long breath of relief when this danger was past, and we found ourselves again, for a brief space only, enjoying the solitude of the river, and the silence of its forest banks.

It was but a short timed enjoyment, however, for as we drifted past a low, swampy island, we were all startled by a most unearthly war-cry, and we just caught a glimpse of shining spears and knives, as several canoes darted along under the lee of an island bank, and disappeared the next instant behind another island.   I arranged everything as well as possible to withstand an attack, for I expected to come to close quarters by sunset, or, at latest, when the darkness closed in.

It was in this country the natives attacked poor Walter Deane at night, when on his way to take command of the Stanley Falls Station, in 1885.   He had drawn his small steamer alongside the bank, as the custom is, while the crew had been employed in cutting up dry wood—fuel for next day's burning.   Wearied with this exertion, all slept soundly—the men scattered about the camp-fires, Deane himself lying under the shade of a neighboring tree—when a thunderstorm, accompanied by the usual deluge of rain, put out the fires and caused every man to think only of his own personal discomforts, the sentry among the number.   Under cover of the darkness and confusion which ensued, the natives of the district, who had been watching their opportunity from the forest, attacked the party—speared several of the surprised soldiers, and wounded Deane himself, ere any of the men recovered from their panic, or were able to fire their rifles at their hidden assailants. Those sleeping on board the steamer, being removed from the confusion and panic on shore, were able, by a timely fusilade, to repel the attack, and the natives were driven back, leaving more than one of Deane's soldiers mortally wounded, and himself so severely hurt that he was forced to return to Stanley Pool, where for several months he lingered in great danger.

It was among these people I now found myself, and every time we passed an island I expected an onslaught, for they were following parallel to us, and we could hear their war-drums behind the forest trees.

The sun was terrifically hot, and the glare on the water was blinding. Soon we got sight of a number of armed natives in their canoes, under the shadow of an opposite island. Shaking their spears at us, they cried : " Arabs, Arabs, we will fight you," and answered all our assurances of friendship with derisive howls.

A little lower down the river we came to a recent forest clearing, where the natives had built a temporary village, consisting of about fifty or sixty conical grass huts. Upon the bank, partly sheltered by the trunks of fallen trees, some two or three hundred men were crouching, armed with their knives, spears and shields. We drifted past them at the distance of about twenty yards ; they would not answer our salutations ; then simultaneously they rushed to the river bank, and stood in an attitude for hurling their spears ; they stamped on the ground, and did not heed me as I uncovered my head and saluted them, assuring them that I was a white man and desired to be their friend. Two heavy spears were thrown at us, which happily fell short of their mark ; undaunted, I held up a couple of brass rods, the currency of the country, and the chief, a great, powerful savage, with a fluttering feather head dress, covered with metal ornaments, said, shaking his spear :

"You lie, you are Arabs ; you will not deceive us with your brass rods; neither will we deceive you with our spears."

This speech was backed up with roars of defiance from his companions, and several more spears were hurled, but these, also, failed to reach us, and as I was unwilling to be the first to shed blood, we pushed on as quickly as might be, refraining from using our rifles.

War-drums and ivory war-horns resounded on both sides of the river as we entered the savage Monungeri district.

The people of this district, inhabiting the two sides of a narrow channel, between wooded islands, had some time before this been chastised by the Congo State Government, for acts of hostility to a passing steamer, and had suffered severely in the conflict. Although defeated and forced to abandon their villages for the time, they had since returned to their former habitations; and no formal "palaver" having been held between the officials of the State and the chiefs of the district, nor a settlement of the dispute effected, the people were as bitterly hostile to the passage of any strangers through their territory as before the fight. Strange to say, I passed through this dreaded channel unperceived, in the darkness, and by midnight we had emerged upon wider stretches of river, where we breathed more freely, for the worst part of our journey, as far as hostile natives were concerned, was now over.

As we paddled along, past a long line of destroyed villages, the charred structures of the grass huts and the bare, burnt fronds of the palm trees stood out in bold relief against the clear night sky.

A short time before, the Arabs had descended the Itimbiri River, which empties into the Congo a few miles below these villages, and had attacked the natives, killing a large number and capturing many prisoners, whom, in due course, they traded for ivory in the remoter inland villages. We continually called in salutation : "Sen-né-né, Sen-né-né, Sen-né-né, né-né," but received no answer, although we frequently heard the rustling of leaves and the snapping of twigs, which plainly indicated the presence of natives. Finally a threatening voice from the distant forest shouted :

"Kenda-mboli, kenda-mboli," ("Go away, go away !")

STANDING ERECT ON THE PLATFORM AT THE STERN OF THE CANOE WAS THE CHIEF

CHAPTER VI.

AT dawn we caught sight of numbers of canoes laden with women and children crossing hurriedly to the forest islands.

We called to them not to fear, saying: "We are Stanley's children;" but they only grew more excited and hurried away all the faster to shelter. Presently a big war-canoe approached us, propelled by about fifty armed warriors, who paddled standing, half the number using their long bladed paddles on each side. Standing erect on the platform at the stern of the canoe, was the chief, a tall, powerfully built man. His feather head-dress fluttered in the wind; on one arm rested his shield, and in his hand he held a large bladed spear. His body was covered with red ochre, produced from powdered cam-wood and palm oil; and wild cat skins hung suspended from his waist. Dashing up alongside us, within twenty yards, they stopped, and the chief said:

"You lie, you are Arabs. See the white cloth on your heads. Stanley's children do not travel like the Arabs. You want meat, you come to catch and eat us; but we are ready for you."

Then howling to intimidate us, they circled round us, several men meanwhile poising their spears to throw at us. Other war-canoes, full of warriors, came to meet and insult us during the half-day it occupied to drift past their country, but none ventured upon an open assault, and we were content to suffer their insults in silence. We were unable to paddle, as it was necessary that all the men should be in readiness with their guns, in case of the attacks which were so frequently threatened.

Drifting closer to the shore at a spot where the fugitive natives had built a temporary village, a small canoe, containing three evil-looking savages, one of whom held a bunch of green bananas, ostensibly for sale, boldly came out to meet us. Fearing treachery, as I caught sight of their spears at the bottom of the canoe, I reached out my hand to place my rifle in a more convenient position. The natives on the bank, who were keenly watching all our movements, immediately commenced to yell and roar at us; the three men plunged into the water and swam ashore, and the people, following in crowds along the bank, threatened us with their spears, and kept up a continuous howling that almost deafened us.

The next day at noon, some few miles below the mouth of the Itimbiri River, we came to a large village, and found the people particularly excited at our arrival, and indulging in hostile demonstrations as they hurried hither and thither among the banana trees lining the top of the bank, through the broad leaves of which their brightly polished spear and knife blades glanced and shone as they caught the sunlight. Presently my attention was drawn to a man beckoning us to land, while in his hand he held up bananas and long sticks of ripe sugar-cane.

We were so greatly in need of food that I decided on venturing ashore, although I had misgivings as to the nature of the reception likely to be accorded us. In a few moments our canoes grounded on the beach, and we were hesitating whether to land or not, when from a clump of bushes on our left rushed a crowd of armed men, yelling frantically and brandishing their weapons as they drew near. We had just time to push off into the stream to avoid a conflict ; and as we drifted off, making what use of our paddles we could, their howls of disappointed rage echoed in our ears.

We were not sorry when the channel through which we were passing opened out into a wider stretch of river, extending in places away to the horizon, and enabling us to obtain a magnificent view of the broad bosom of the river, tranquil and calm, flowing on around the numerous islands, whose serrated crowns of distant tree-tops rose against the hazy sky line.

On this broad expanse we observed a big canoe coming towards us, containing about forty armed men, several of them with guns. We stopped paddling in order to be prepared for them should they attack us ; but on drawing near I discovered them to be a party of Bangala natives, belonging to a post of the Congo State that had been established a few months before at Yambinga, a village near by, to keep an eye upon the movements of the Arabs on the Itimbiri River, and with a view to imposing order upon the turbulent natives of the district, and winning them over to a system of good behavior.

I now learned that in endeavoring to effect this latter object it had been found necessary by the Belgian officer commanding the post to engage in hostilities a few days previously, with the very people whose village we were now approaching. As a result of the conflict, the garrison of Yambinga post had been " boycotted," and the canoe load of natives I had met were now on their way to purchase food in villages which had not suffered during the recent fight.

In the evening, soon after sunset, we reached the populous

village of Bumba, where our appearance seemed to cause great
consternation. We repeatedly called the chief, with whom I was
acquainted, but the yells and shouts and beating of alarm drums
prevented him from hearing us. We drifted past the village about
one hundred yards out in the stream, the thick cloud of smoke
from the village fires hanging over the river bank preventing us
from seeing anything; while from the dense obscurity the shouts
and yells of the frightened people rising above the din of the drums
produced a weird effect.

Later on, several big canoes, with armed men in them,
cautiously approached us, and a gruff voice hailed us in the darkness, saying :

"What do you want with our chief ? You are of the people of
the white man of Yambinga, who fought us three days ago. Go
away quickly ; we are not friends."

Thus everywhere our friendly intentions were doubted. Higher
up the river, where to have been recognized as a white man would
have carried some sense of security with it, we were mistaken for
Arabs ; while here, the very fact of my being a white man induced
the natives to doubt my overtures of friendship ; they, naturally
enough, connecting my advent on the scene of their recent defeat,
at the hands of the Belgian officer, with that unfortunate event.
There was nothing for it but to continue our journey.

We passed several small villages during the night, causing great
confusion among the disturbed inhabitants in the darkness;
women and children screamed and cried as they rushed to the
forest for shelter, and the men's voices, as they shouted the alarm
of danger, echoed far across the placid river.

The following day we drifted past picturesque islets, and I shot
several ibises with my rifle, my men diving in the river, regardless

of crocodiles, to recover them. Troops of monkeys sported playfully among the branches of the high forest trees, and the sharp crack of a rifle-shot seemed to awaken the vast woods; monkeys chattered and barked, great horn-bills clattered as they flew from tree to tree, in apparent annoyance at being disturbed, whilst numberless little sun birds fluttered about from one orchid to another, giving life and movement to the scene.

The following day the sun was exceedingly hot, and we drifted lazily through narrow channels bordered by forest and swamp, without seeing any sign of natives. I lay in the bottom of the biggest canoe, my head aching

from the excessive heat, and I tried in vain to read some theological controversies in a Christian newspaper called the *British Weekly*, which I found in the bottom of a case of provisions kindly given me, more than a year before, by the Rev. Charles Ingham, a missionary on the Lower Congo. Perhaps the subject was too profound for my clouded intelligence, or perhaps it was that the heat enervated my reasoning power, for, after reading the same paragraphs over and over again, I became quite confused in the maze of the many-syllabled words used by the ecclesiastical gentlemen to illustrate their intricate theories.

Several times during the day we heard the gruff barks of chimpanzees in the forest, but were unable to get a sight at their child-like faces, as they hurried off deeper into the woods at our approach. In the evening, we came in view of the Oupoto Hills. Since my previous journey, eleven months before, the Bopoto people, after being severely punished by the officers of the Congo Free State for unruly behavior and an attack upon a party of State soldiers, were now very friendly disposed towards white men. Indeed, it appears to be absolutely necessary, in dealing with these savage tribes, in the beginning, to inspire them with the sentiment of fear and a deep respect for your fighting powers. I visited a small stockaded village at the lower end of the Bopoto district, and hurrying ashore, commenced sketching their types and figures before the natives could realize my intentions. I drew a few heads of the natives in my sketch book, bought some eggs and a cannibal necklace of human teeth, and resumed my journey again, all within the space of half an hour. In a forest, just below this village, I shot a very large, brown monkey, which my two Niam-Niams consumed with evident relish in an astonishingly brief time, and no doubt feeling exceedingly "good" after having successfully concluded the operation. We continued paddling along until midnight, when we were overtaken by a terrific thunderstorm. We made the canoes fast alongside the forest bank just to leeward of a big dead tree that lay out in the river; the water became so rough and the wind so violent that it appeared as though we should inevitably be swamped. The night was dark, except when occasional vivid flashes of lightning showed us up in all our huddled wretchedness. Growing weary at last of sitting awake, waiting for the storm to cease, I lay down in the bottom of the bigger canoe to sleep, exposed to the wind and rain, being so thoroughly exhausted I scarcely cared what might happen to us. I awoke at dawn, cold, stiff and shivering, and found that I had been lying in a pool of water several inches deep. The storm had passed, and my men were huddled together in little groups, pictures of misery. One of my Niam-Niams was sitting naked, with his loin-cloth bound around his head, for he said his head was sick. My note books and sketch books, and in fact all my belongings, were drenched and thrown into a dripping heap, to await the appearance of the sun to dry them.

In describing the characteristics of my crew, I would class my servant, "Msa," of Zanzibar, first. He was bright, active and faithful. Next in merit I would rank "Makatuku," a thick-lipped freeman, whose mother was a native of Yao. He was always cheerful, ready for any emergency, powerful and active, and very much attached to "Msa;" they used to eat out of the same dish. Old "Juma bin Abdullah Suza" came from Madagascar. He invariably wore an old tarpaulin "sou'-wester;" was very fond of smoked fish, and was a true type of a dusky Don Juan among the cannibal belles. "Mzee Bilalli" was sold as a slave when quite a boy, by his tribe, to the Arab slave dealers on Lake Nyassa, with

whom he had spent most of his life. On the march he always carried the heaviest load, and he was never idle ; when not otherwise
engaged, he would be carefully tying tobacco leaves in a small
package, or with grass threads sewing up the rents in his ragged
loin-cloth. " Shomali " was a great, fat, lazy slave, ready to sleep
upon the least provocation. " Khamici " (Thursday) was useless
when any work had to be done, but at all other times he was
active, and quite a dandy. " Nobi Demici " was also a slave ; he
had little brains, but a capacious appetite. Little " Mabruki " was
a sharp, shrewd boy, with a very old-fashioned face ; just the
type of boy to pick up a living anywhere. The other members of
my crew were of so little use that they are scarcely worth men-
tioning.

We made but little progress that day, on account of the strong
head-wind, and at sunset there was every indication of another
thunderstorm ; it passed away, however, by midnight, and the
moon shone brightly. In one place we were carried away by the
swift current and swept into the forest bank ; the canoes nearly
capsized, and we were all very much torn with thorns. At daylight I was suddenly aroused by Makatuku, who said, in a hoarse
whisper :

" Bwana, Amka ! Amka ! Kuona Ntembo !" (Master, wake
up ! See ! there is an elephant !) and close ahead of us, within a
few yards, was a large elephant climbing up the slippery bank
after his morning bath. I fired with my express rifle and struck
him in the head ; he roared with pain, and fell back into the
water, splashing us with spray. As he recovered himself, I fired
again, but, unfortunately, with bad aim, striking him in the
shoulder. Quickly inserting two more cartridges I shot him
again in the head, and he fell heavily on the bank, apparently

dead. Hastily paddling our unwieldy canoes to the bank, I jumped ashore, sinking up to my arm-pits in black mud, and, while endeavoring to extricate myself, I became entangled in the branches of a dead tree. In the meantime, the wounded elephant

had staggered to his feet, and, trumpeting shrilly in agony, he made off into the forest, crashing through the dense undergrowth. Floundering ashore I hurried after him, but soon came to deep swamp and almost impassable jungle. I followed his tracks for a short distance, but the wounded beast, mustering up all his dying strength, had got away; and although I endeavored to continue, I soon found the task impossible, and was reluctantly compelled to abandon the chase. All was silent in the forest except the skurrying of chattering monkeys, as they jumped from one swinging branch to another.

I returned to my canoes, with my clothes torn to shreds, and my body sorely scratched from the thorny scrub. This little episode afforded my men a topic for conversation during the remainder of the day; they grew quite animated when talking of the meat we had lost, and graphically mimicked the contortions of the poor wounded elephant after each shot.

The two following days and nights passed without incident, until suddenly, late in the afternoon, we heard a voice saying, ironically :

" Benu kuieba te kuruka," (You people don't know how to paddle) ; and looking up, I saw a fine, handsome Bangala woman, attired in a grass skirt, with polished brass necklace and bracelets, standing with her arms folded in a most graceful attitude on the forest bank, partly hidden in the dark olive-green foliage. The sudden appearance of this figure, after so long an absence of natives, and her calm remark, struck us all as being very ludicrous.

ARUIMI TYPE.

CHAPTER VII.

THE next day we saw several women paddling canoes on the river, but they would not approach us, saying: "Our men are away at war." I subsequently discovered that about a thousand men of the Mobeka tribe had gone up river, in sixty war canoes, to fight the people of Oupoto. They must have passed us the previous night, taking another channel, so that we did not see them. About midnight I reached the camp of Monsieur Hodister, an agent of the Belgian Trading Company. He was most hospitable, and entertained me until the early hours of the morning by relating incidents that had occurred during his residence among the Mobeka people. Such confidence had Hodister inspired among these people that they intrusted their women to his care during their absence on the war expedition against Oupoto ; and I found numbers of the female relatives of the departed warriors congregated around his station, implicitly believing in his power to defend them.

Leaving Hodister's early the next morning, and drifting past the long line of Mobeka villages, the women crowded along the banks of the river, asking eagerly if we could give them news of the result of the war with Oupoto. The only men to be seen were

T

invalids and cripples, for every able-bodied man had gone to fight.

The two following days were uneventful; four of my men were helplessly ill with colds, rheumatism and fever, brought on from exposure to the cold, miasmatic fogs by night, and the fierce tropical sun by day. My health was also bad, and the scratches and cuts which I re-

ceived two days be-fore during my un successful elephant hunt, had become inflamed and fester-ing sores. Of all of my crew, the big black monkey seem-ed to be most in his element, his appe-tite rivaling that of the Niam-Niams, who, by the longing glances they often cast upon his bulky proportions, I could see, thought it a

A BANGALA VILLAGE SCENE.

terrible waste of plantains and bananas on my part to give them to a monkey, when both monkey and plantains—not to mention bananas as a "dressing"—might form such a noble repast for two poor, hungry Niam-Niams.

Upon reaching Bangala, I found there had been war between the natives of some villages in that district and the Congo State.

"STREAKS OF FIRE REACHED FORTH FROM EACH SIDE."

Several of the State buildings had been destroyed, and a soldier of the garrison, who had been speared to death, had been dug up two days after his burial, by the hostile natives, who ate the corpse. During the short time I remained in the State Station at Bangala, one of the hostile chiefs came to tender his submission, and he paid meekly the fine imposed upon him by the State representative, which consisted of two thousand brass rods, two large canoes and two slaves, representing a value of from £150 to £200 sterling.

Until long past midnight, we drifted past the watch-fires of the natives, and heard their alarm drums echoing from side to side of the river; however, we were not interfered with. At about 3 A. M. it became very foggy, and we met with an accident that nearly ended disastrously. The swift current swept us upon a formidable snag, and swinging broadside to the stream, we shipped a quantity of water. The following night we were caught in a fierce tornado, and had to remain holding fast to the bank, surging and rolling about in the waves, drenched and miserable, until daylight. The united efforts of half my men were necessary, continually bailing out the water, to save us from being swamped.

Owing to fresh cases of sickness, I was left with only five able-bodied men to paddle our two great, heavy canoes, three by day and two by night; we consequently did no more than drift with the current, and made most erratic attempts at steering when thus at the mercy of the stream. About an hour before sunset, the change in the color of the water indicated our vicinity to the Lulungu river, and suddenly, as we passed an islet, we came in view of hundreds of native huts in flames. Great clouds of smoke rose up in an unbroken column; smouldering trees lay everywhere along the river bank, and in the distance we heard a heavy fusillade of guns. Several big war-canoes shot past us, propelled by warriors attired in all their war-paint. In answer to my inquiries they bluffly replied : That it was a little affair of their own; that they did not want any interference from me, and that if we did not keep farther out from the river bank, we might be accidentally shot.

Drifting past the burning villages, at a distance of about fifty yards from the river bank, we obtained a splendid view of the fight. Some four hundred painted and befeathered fighting men were engaged on each side, almost hand to hand, in a thick patch of banana trees. Streaks of fire belched forth from each side, followed by loud reports ; in the meantime, dusky forms could be distinguished through the thick smoke, rushing backwards and forwards to reload their flintlock guns. The burning villages extended along the river bank for upwards of two miles ; and as the sunset and the short tropical twilight were followed by dense darkness, the flames of the blazing huts, the bright flashes from the guns, illuminating for an instant the rolling cloud of smoke which rose over the scene of destruction, until it hung in the air a mountain of deeper darkness than the night, all reflected in the placid river, formed, indeed, an impressive spectacle.

Old Juma remarked that this was "a fighting moon ;" and, indeed, we had passed through little else but scenes of war since quitting the Aruimi River, hundreds of miles above this point.

Two nights afterwards, we were assaulted by a hippopotamus, who charged our canoes amidship, breaking adrift the lashings with which the two canoes were secured together, and causing us considerable inconvenience. The night was beautifully clear, the sky a blaze of twinkling stars. Nothing of interest occurred until daylight the next morning, when we received another crashing bump from a hippopotamus, whilst I was shaving. After a bullet

from my rifle, the beast retired hastily into deep water. A little later we passed along a narrow channel, in the midst of hundreds of hippopotami. One old bull exhibited such a countenance of defiance to us that I was compelled to shoot him.

At noon we saw two big bull hippopotami, whose bodies would compare in circumference with an average elephant's, fighting on a sand-bank. The monsters rushed at each other with their immense jaws wide open, and gored one another with their formidable tusks; then, rising on their hind legs, and dashing their massive heads together, they fell heavily on the sand. Recovering themselves, they would recede a few paces, and charging one another again, the clash of their meeting tusks and the grunts of rage, snorting the bloody sand from their nostrils, could be distinctly heard as they reared up on their hind legs, only to fall back again. We watched the encounter for upwards of half an hour, until the gigantic brutes, all gored, bloody and covered with froth, fought their way into deep water and disappeared in a perfect sea of foam and spray, the troubled waters plashing up in waves on the sand-bank they had quitted.

Later on, we passed several groups of natives, who were engaged in burning grass-stalks for the preparation of potash salt. They rushed away into the forest, frightened at such an unwonted sight as a white man and his party drifting down the river in two such big canoes. They evidently thought that something serious had happened to cause me to undertake a journey in such a craft.

Soon after another heavy thunderstorm drenched us. After getting things settled again, I lay down to rest, and my servant, Msa, came with my old iron kettle to pour out a cup of hot coffee. Suddenly, within three or four yards of us, a great hippopotamus rose up out of the water, with open jaws, grunting savagely; he sank back into the water again, and the next instant he had charged us from below, splitting the small canoe almost from end to end. Msa was thrown against me, and the boiling coffee scalded us both ; the canoe lashings were carried away ; four men were thrown into the water, and in the confusion and darkness I mistook their black shadows in the water for the irate hippopotamus, and was just about to fire, when I recognized old Juma, as he spluttered :

" Tu na-ona, tabu, sana bwana," (What a time we are having).

We paddled ashore, and were occupied the remainder of the night repairing the damages. What with the exposure to the fierce heat of the sun by day, and to the chilling dew of the nights, during the twenty-two days we had been cooped up in this rickety old craft, not to speak of the numerous tornadoes and the drenching down-pours of rain we had continually experienced, or the miseries of bad food and little of it, we were all now heartily sick of the journey, and anxious only to reach our destination.

We worked away with a will at the task of repairing the canoes, and were able early next morning to continue our journey.

As we approached the upper villages of the populous district of Bolobo, I found the people in a state of great excitement ; some were madly dancing, others uttering wails of lament, for the old chief, " Ibaka " had died some seven days before, and he had been interred that day ; three of his wives being buried alive with the corpse. They had already decapitated six slaves, and an execution of another of these poor wretches had just occurred a few minutes before my arrival ; indeed, the children were still mimicking the ghastly twitchings of the poor victim's features after the head had been cut off. Other slaves were yet to suffer, for Ibaka had been a great chief, and must enter the next world with a suitable retinue.

"AND THE NEXT INSTANT HE HAD CHARGED US FROM BELOW."

As we left Bolobo, a fair wind sprang up, and I hoisted my old blanket as an impromptu sail. We made good progress in this way, and the poor, worn-out Zanzibaris lay back in the bottoms of the canoes and gazed admiringly upon the old red blanket, which was blown out like a balloon. Old Juma Abdallah Suza said that this mode of traveling reminded him of dhow life on the Zanzibar coast. Bilalli, who was carefully binding up a tobacco leaf in his loin cloth, nodded his head in assent. Presently, the old blanket, being no longer able to stand the strain, quietly parted up the middle. The wind increased, and we tossed and rolled about in the waves until I expected every moment a catastrophe. To add to our discomfiture, the banks were lined with ugly black rocks, over which the waves dashed into white foam. Everything was drenched; the few fowls I carried for provisions cackled with fright, and the Zanzibaris' countenances assumed an anxious expression; they all stripped off their loin cloths, ready for an emergency.

"Just like an old dhow at sea," remarked old Juma, as he tied his sou'-wester into a little ball, which he strung round his waist for safe-keeping. Fortunately we soon reached the mud bank of a deserted village. Carrying everything ashore, we camped for the night, cold and wet. Before we slept, however, we received the intelligence from a fisherman, who passed by in a canoe, that we were in a village that had been deserted on account of the hostilities of the two neighboring villages on either side; that the warfare still continued, and that we should probably see trouble during the night. Despite this by no means comforting assurance, we stretched our weary limbs on heaps of fresh-cut grass, beneath the dilapidated and smoky roofs of the abandoned village, taking the necessary precaution to post sentinels, who could give the alarm if danger threatened. Upon awakening the next morning, we found that the storm had passed, and the sky was cloudless.

Hurriedly roasting a few ears of maize for our breakfast, we again embarked, and, freshened by our night's rest, we paddled along quite cheerfully, and, early in the afternoon of the second day, we espied a small steamer lying alongside the forest bank. The native crew were busily engaged cutting firewood for fuel, and the blows of their axes echoed across the river as we drew near. I was delighted to find that the steamer was in charge of my old friends, E. J. Glave and T. Thompson, whom I had not seen for a considerable time. They were on their way up to explore the Ruki River. We camped together that night, relating the different adventures that had befallen us since our last meeting, and I enjoyed a good dinner, washed down with a glass of wine, after the scanty fare of our long voyage.

The following morning, after hearty hand shakes, we resumed our respective journeys, and I reached my destination, Stanley Pool, the next evening, a few hours after dark, having covered a distance of 1,100 miles in twenty-seven days and nights, my crew consisting of six able-bodied men, four invalids and three boys. This completed my canoe journeying upon the Congo, the total distance so traversed being 2,500 miles.

From Stanley Pool we marched overland fifteen days, and upon reaching the coast I received instructions from the Emin Pasha Relief committee to embark for London with my twelve Zanzibaris, who would be forwarded from thence to Zanzibar *via* the Suez Canal.

The first steamer leaving Banana for Europe was the *Afrikaan*, belonging to the Dutch Trading Co., bound for Rotterdam. This steamer brings supplies to the merchants, and missionaries to the natives, and on the return voyage, the sailors, taking advantage of the absence of passengers, carry home whole troops of chattering monkeys, and hang cages filled with screeching parrots in every part of the ship, a noisy combination which renders the homeward voyage lively to an irritating degree.

It was Sunday when we arrived at the old city of Rotterdam, where the citizens, in their Sunday attire, crowded the quays to catch a glimpse of the strange group of Zanzibaris gathered on the forecastle of the African steamer. The London steamer was just on the point of starting, and I hurried my dazed followers across quays and over several bridges, and placed them on board the English boat. Before leaving, I procured twelve suits of rough blue serge, as it was necessary that they should appear in London with something more respectable than the ragged loin cloths they had worn during the voyage. We made our way up the Thames in fog and rain. As the men were anxious to see the strange wonders of the white man's country, they stood in the rain and were consequently drenched. I overheard one of them say that he should be glad when they landed so that he might bathe in the river.

"But you can't bathe in this river Thames as you did in the Congo," said I.

"Well, master, what are we to do?" and opening his shirt he said, "for we are all blue."

It appeared that being thoroughly wet by the rain, the dye had come out of the cheap sailor clothing, and had stained their skins a sky blue.

At Blackwall I placed my men in an emigrants' home, and a few days afterwards they were on the deck of a British India steamer bound for Zanzibar—and thus on the 4th of July, 1889, I parted with my simple, faithful followers. We had seen many adventures, and shared many hardships together. Their devotion had been tested by severe trials, and now the remembrance of their kindness and patience only remained, and I forgot their faults and failings. Standing on the jetty while the vessel was slowly moving out of the dock, I could not suppress a feeling of sadness, as, grouped on the deck, my Zanzibaris, waving their ragged turbans, shouted a last farewell, "Kwa heri! Kwa heri bwana wangu (good-bye, my master, good bye!)"

PRINTED BY
SPOTTISWOODE AND CO., NEW-STREET SQUARE
LONDON